About the author

Scenarist, columnist, academic and humorist, Leo Rosten was a writer of remarkable versatility. The author of countless books on every subject: Hollywood, politics, sociology and painting, he was most famous for his humorous writings: his affectionate compendium *The Joys of Yiddish* and, of course, the Hyman Kaplan books. These began as a series of sketches he wrote while studying for his PhD and were first published in *The New Yorker* under the name Leonard Q Ross. After graduating from the University of Chicago (he was also a night school instructor for two years while in Chicago) and the London School of Economics, he taught political science at the Universities of Yale, California and Columbia. He lived in New York until his death in 1997.

The Return of
H*Y*M*A*N
K*A*P*L*A*N

PRION HUMOUR CLASSICS

* for copyright reasons these titles are not available in the USA or Canada in the Prion edition.

The Return of
H∗Y∗M∗A∗N
K∗A∗P∗L∗A∗N

LEO ROSTEN

with a new introduction by
HOWARD JACOBSON

PRION

Originally published in 1959
This edition published by Prion Books Ltd in 2000
Reprinted 2003 by

Prion
an imprint of the
Carlton Publishing Group
20 Mortimer Street
London W1T 3JW

Copyright © Leo C. Rosten 1959
Published in Great Britain by arrangement with
Constable Publishers, London
Introduction copyright © Howard Jacobson 2000

A catalogue record for this book is available from the
British Library

ISBN 1-85375-391-2

Jacket design by Jon Gray
Jacket image courtesy of Hulton Getty

Printed in Great Britain
by Mackays

To Madeline and Peggy

Grateful acknowlegment is made to *The New Yorker* and *Harper's Magazine*, where several of these stories first appeared.

Contents

INTRODUCTION

by HOWARD JACOBSON

The Education of H∗Y∗M∗A∗N K∗A∗P∗L∗A∗N is one of those little books that makes you wonder why you ever spent so much time on *War and Peace*. For whatever isn't in H∗Y∗M∗A∗N K∗A∗P∗L∗A∗N you feel, isn't worth knowing.

It's an illusion, of course. But then all books are illusions and the best writers, in the end, are those who leave you guessing how they've done it. *The Education of* H∗Y∗M∗A∗N K∗A∗P∗L∗A∗N, published originally as stories in *The New Yorker* and subsequently in a single volume in 1937 – note the date, the date's important – was followed up in 1959 – that date's important too – by *The Return of* H∗Y∗M∗A∗N K∗A∗P∗L∗A∗N. Then that was that. Now you saw them, now you didn't. Enough already, as every good illusionist knows. After which Leo Rosten became best known for *The Joys of Yiddish* the friendliest, funniest, and most useful lexicon ever written. But not as funny, for nothing is as funny, as the H∗Y∗M∗A∗N K∗A∗P∗L∗A∗N books.

For my money – though I know there are those who think otherwise – the second is not quite so successful as the first. Nothing serious: it tries a little harder, that's all. And that's bound to be the case when you return to something which is already perfect. But there's another reason, I think, for the infinitesimal falling-off – the War has happened. In other words, it now puts a greater strain on credulity to accept that all of life is contained within the walls of the American Night Preparatory School for Adults ("English – Americanization – Civics – Preparation for Naturalization"). There always was, of course, an unspoken history of fraught migration in the nightly assemblage of Mitnicks and Fishbeins and Caravellos, eager now to acquire the linguistics (forever impossible in Kaplan's case) of being an American; but nothing of the poverty or persecution that brought them to America in the first place ever needed to be spelt out. Having fled here from wherever, the new citizens could shelter from the storm, victims solely of the cruelties of English grammar. Outside, the elements raged –

> The March rain slithered across the windows. it was a nasty night, a night of wet feet, drab spirits, and head colds

– raged the more furiously, sometimes, as a sort of panic measure induced by the wilder flights of Hyman Kaplan's reasoning –

> The recess bell rang. And the raindrops, conscious of their destiny, howled on the steamy windows, like madmen.

But within, the madness was only in men's minds. Before 1937 some semblance of innocence could still be believed in. Hyman Kaplan himself almost typified it. Thereafter, innocence becomes a tougher proposition.

This is not to say that Hyman Kaplan's benignity, his unsurpassing good nature, was ever merely saintly. The

American Night Preparatory School for Adults is not a gathering place for holy fools. Throughout all his fiery encounters with the basic laws of English grammar and the fundamentals of American History, he never forgets that he has his pride to think about, his position as philosopher and philologist to consider, and scores to settle with his fellow preparatees. Indeed, one of the great joys of these stories is his long-running entanglement – so long-running it amounts almost to a romance – with the class's most accomplished but most diffident student, Miss Rose Mitnick, referred to always by Hyman Kaplan, with a bluntness which only devotion can explain, as plain Mitnick. In his own words, spelling and metrical form

> Critisising Mitnick
> Is a picnick

Once launched, there is an unstoppable quality to Hyman Kaplan's flow of misspellings, mispronunciations, mispunctuations, misconceptions, Malapropisms, and the like. As a lexicographer of genius himself, Leo Rosten delights in an invention who appears to be forever giving him the slip, perpetrating such liberties on the language that it is hard not to feel that an entirely new, not to say better, language is unfolding before our eyes. "For Mr Kaplan was no ordinary student ... In his peculiar linguistic universe there was the germ of a new lexicography." A claim which no one who has read Hyman Kaplan declining the verb to fail – "fail, failed, bankrupt" – or spelling pencil-sharpener, "pantsil-chopner", or venturing, as the superior form of "good", "high-cless", would dream of refuting.

Introduction

A new lexicography of feeling, too. Only think of Kaplan apologizing to Mr Parkhill for being perhaps a little too florid in his appreciation of him – "Maybe de spitch I rad vas too formmal. But avery void I said – it came fromm below mine heart!"

Hilarious as these night class solecisms are, and wonderful as they look on the page – gorgeous blooms of typographical miscreation and erroneousness, all of them – we never laugh from the position of those who know better. Think of Hyman Kaplan's extravagances as "mistakes" and we miss the value of him. Would we really want to correct the astounding and profound topography of "below mine heart"? In favour of what? From the bottom of?

Leo Rosten means it when he attributes to the conventional, slow-witted Mr Parkhill, the dawning realization that his worst pupil, Hyman Kaplan, is "a remarkable man." Set anyone foreign to a language the task of familarizing himself with it, and you will have occasional remarkable effects. We think afresh when we think in a grammar not native to us. Thus, other beginners may have stumbled, with almost as much felicity as Kaplan, around the geography of the heart. But it takes a man of unusually deep feeling to go on sounding, as Hyman Kaplan does, the poetry of inaccuracy and misuse.

Rosten's own English, meanwhile, maintains a beautiful poise, as though keeping its head in a shipwreck. "Mr Kaplan stopped, his hand in mid-air," he tells us, "like a gull coasting." Much of the drollery comes from this maintenance, against the odds, of a sort of distraught precision. "The smile on the face of Mr

Kaplan" we learn, "had taken on something beatific and imperishable." Beatific, in that context, any old satirist may have come up with. Imperishable is the mark of someone working at the highest level of comic writing.

And that's because it both is funny – suggesting a fearful eternity, if you are destined to go on teaching Mr Kaplan – and is not. For Hyman Kaplan's spirit truly is imperishable. In the annals of indomitableness he lives with Falstaff and Micawber. But he is the more remarkable for being, as they are not, a long way from his linguistic home. So we see him inventing his own imperishability, as it were from scratch, in language. To enjoy the greatest *coup de théatre* in all literature, for irrefutable proof, once and for all, of the unconquerable imagination of man, read Hyman Kaplan confounding those would confound him, those who would dare pick out the grammatic absurdity of a sentence in a letter to his uncle – "'If your eye falls on a bargain please pick it up?' Som English, Mr Kaplan!"– with the dazzling revelation that Hyman had written precisely what he had meant to write, for the reason that his uncle had a glass-eye.

Preface
The Confessions of
Mr. Parkhill

Mr. Kaplan was born one Sunday night, over twenty years ago, quite unexpectedly and full-grown as Athene, to an earnest young man who was lost in solemn research for a book about the Washington correspondents. The earnest young man, who was bucking for his Ph.D., was also an innocent young man. Because he was pining to take the academic vows (poverty, bibliography, and jargon), he signed that first story about Mr. Kaplan "Leonard Q. Ross," a pure figment of reason. For the young man was afraid of what his professors might do if they discovered that whilst he was living in Washington on an honorific fellowship, he was spending his weekends in his secret vice—the writing of fiction. Worse, that fiction contained humor.

The earnest and innocent young man had not the faintest notion of writing a second story about Mr. Kaplan. It was, for one thing, much too difficult. It was, for another, much too unpromising. After all, Grammar, Spelling, and Pronunciation are hardly dramatic personae; and the locale could scarcely be less inspiring: a classroom, a classroom of a beginners' grade, a classroom of a beginners' grade in a night school, a classroom of a beginners' grade in a night school for adults, a classroom of a beginners' grade in a night school for adults presided over not by a rich, juicy character, such as Samuel Johnson or Scaramouche, but by a terribly staid teacher named Parkhill.

No, no, a second story, strapped within so many strait jackets to the imagination, was not even dreamed of by the clandestine author of the first.

But that first story had already been written. Mr. Kaplan *existed*. He had, in fact, taken up residence in the soul of the earnest and innocent young man— unbidden, unencouraged—and was acting as if he held a first mortgage on the place.

For characters who have been flung into orbit within the inner galaxies of the self soon exert a curious tyranny over their creators, and before long the earnest and innocent young man in Washington found himself writing a second story about Mr. Kaplan, then a third, and a fourth, until, an exhilarated but helpless caboose to a roaring comet, he had written enough stories about Mr. Parkhill and his pilgrims to divert the editors and readers of *The New Yorker* for several years running.

After that, it was impossible to keep Mr. Kaplan from what had apparently been his purpose all along— life within the covers of a book. The title, suggested by a publisher who had a score to settle with Henry Adams, was *The Education of* H*Y*M*A*N K*A*P*L*A*N. The rest is misery.

I am, of course, that once earnest and innocent young (once) man. For twenty years I have been haunted, plagued, goaded and berated by the poltergeists of my psyche for nipping them off in the flower of their youth. Perhaps now they will let me live in peace.

In the years since Mr. Kaplan & Company first asserted their peculiar dominion over my life, I have been asked many questions, about him and about myself—by baffled, if not downright suspicious, friends who thought I had a helluva nerve confiding to them that "Leonard Q. Ross" and I were two and the same; by teachers throughout the land who were beginning to talk to themselves because of Kaplans or Caravellos or Pinskys of their own; by entirely innocent students who had been condemned to institutions of learning and were wrestling doomed matches with the cunning and slippery syntax of English; by critics trying to shore up the sea wall between their fantasies and mine; by refugees, from Europe and the Orient, who simply could not believe that anyone not himself a refugee could possibly understand the tortures they had endured studying the language invented by Torque-mada.

I should like to answer some of these questions, as simply and truthfully as I can. Truth is edifying, whole-some, and stranger than fiction. As Mark Twain said, "Why shouldn't it be?" Life, unlike fiction, doesn't have to make either sense or point.

"Are the Hyman Kaplan stories true?"
Yes, they are all true—but they never happened.

"Were you ever a teacher in a night school for adults?"
Yes. I taught (I thought) for about two years, as a bootleg substitute for an instructor in a night school on the West Side of Chicago. I was not an accredited teacher, and have since become a discredited sub-stitute, because my talents, such as they were, had not yet been crippled by Required Courses in Education.

I committed pedagogy for an instructor who had sensibly suffered a nervous breakdown. Wild horses will not drag out of me the name of the school, which I remember with the deepest affection.

"Why did you move the scene from Chicago to New York?"

It seemed natural. It seemed appropriate. It seemed inevitable. Stories about immigrants in a night school just have an irresistible tropism for that marvelous carnival of a city. Besides, New York has an annual mean rainfall.

"Did you actually have a student like Hyman Kaplan?"

No. Life is not that beneficent.

There was put at my mercy, briefly, a student who, had he acted the way he *should* have acted, would have resembled Mr. Kaplan. The student, being only human, never did. (One of my favorite fans is a lady who wrote to me for years, offering treasures withheld by Scheherezade if she could but meet the creator of the man she insisted on calling "Human" Kaplan.)

Mr. Kaplan is, I suppose, the projected image of certain traits of personality, nourished by narcissism and pushed to the outermost boundaries of yearning. A famous psychoanalyst once analyzed Mr. Kaplan and concluded he was my alter ego. I sometimes think it is the other way round.

"Were you Mr. Parkhill?"

I don't know. But I also don't know who else he could have been, or where else he could have come from.

Not all of me, I hasten to add, is Mr. Parkhill, nor all

of him me. Part of him, I suspect, is that portion of me which is conventional, slow-witted, virtuous beyond belief. Other facets of him, which are not me, I deeply envy and admire: infinite patience, kindliness, restraint, an incorruptible faith in man, and unshatterable faith in his perfectibility.

What puzzles me about Mr. Parkhill is that he seems to think that every man and woman on earth can be taught, can learn, can improve, can stand at last before the Throne. I, who have the greatest difficulty in persuading my children that the evidence is all against this, am often accused of being reactionary when I am only trying to be realistic, and am often charged with being cynical when I am only trying to be detached. It has gotten to the point where I open my prayers each morning with two lines from Bertrand Russell: "It has been said that man is a rational animal. All my life I have been searching for evidence which could support this."

"Was there a real Miss Mitnick ?"
Miss Mitnick neither was nor *is* real. I found this sweet, shy maiden, with whom I am madly in love, in a neglected glen of my reveries.

"Do you have a special way of writing?"
Yes. I use a special fountain pen, which I fill with my blood.

"Is it harder to write humor than serious things?"
Yes. God, yes.

"Is dialect harder to write than other forms of humor ?"

Much. It is also more risky, more tricky, more perplexing, and more dangerous.

Humor is the affectionate communication of insight. (Satire is focused bitterness, and burlesque the skewing of proportions.) Humor is, I think, the subtlest and chanciest of literary forms. It is surely not accidental that there are a thousand novelists, essayists, poets, journalists for each humorist. It is a long, long time between James Thurbers.

Comic dialect is humor plus anthropology. Dialect must seduce the eye to reach the ear and be orchestrated in the brain. It must tantalize without irritating, and defer without frustrating. It must carry a visual promise to the reader that what he does not instantly recognize can be deciphered with ease and will be rewarded by pleasure. The reader must be cued into making what he thinks is his own special and private discovery—a discovery of delight which, he suspects, neither the character nor the author fully appreciates.

Dialect is not transcription. Nothing is more depressing than a passage of broken English exactly transcribed from the spoken. The "accurate ear" for which a writer is praised is as inventive as it is accurate. It is creative, not literal, for the writer transforms that which he hears into that which you could not. There is a magic in dialect which can liberate us from the prisons of the familiar.

In the antic freedom of phonetics, mortals say "ship" when they mean the source of wool, or "sheep" when they mean a vessel. Others throw "bet" around with the abandon of a gambler—to mean either "bat," "bet," "bad," or "bed."

The writer must therefore create exact, if camouflaged, contexts within which the reader's responses are firmly controlled. He must convey without explaining. Mr. Kaplan may say "fond mine fife fit don," which suggests a devoted shaft of flutes fit for an Oxford tutor. But if the clues have been properly structured, and the channels of association properly cut, the reader will have to do no heavy lifting to know that Mr. Kaplan, having lost something, found it five feet down.

Or take Mrs. Moskowitz. Poor, dear Mrs. Moskowitz. She says, if I were to record it with absolute rigor, "I hate the brat." But that is not at all what she means. If I made her say, instead, "I ate the brat," which is closer to her message, Mrs. Moskowitz would be tainted with cannibalism, which is absurd. (There are certain *animals* Mrs. Moskowitz would not dream of digesting.) I would have to violate truth, in the service of truth, and write Mrs. Moskowitz's perfectly innocent thought as "I ate the brad." (Why doesn't she say "I ate the bread"? The day she does, I'll promote her to Miss Higby's grade.)

The problem is immensely complicated when the characters in a story write as well as speak. For they write quite differently from the way they speak. Each, indeed, uses two separate vocabularies. Irate Hawkshaws used to write me complaining that on page such-and-such Mr. Kaplan wrote "was," whereas on page tit-for-tat he said "vas." They missed the point: beginners learn to *write* "was" without the slightest anguish, but many pronounce it "vas" until threatened with execution.

There are more, and more mischievous, jokers in this

enchanting deck. Take Mr. Kaplan's name. It is a simple name. Anyone in the class can spell it correctly. But notice: Mr. Kaplan refers to himself as "Keplen," Mr. Blattberg calls him "Kaplen," Mr. Plonsky always bellows "Keplan," Mr. Matsoukas mutters "Koplen," and Olga Tarnova, who could wring lurid overtones from a telephone number, moans "Koplan."

Apart from driving my proof-readers crazy (and any departures from the code above are clearly their doing and not mine), these variations seem to me to add richness to the characterizations, and texture and nuance to the language which Mr. Parkhill's disciples keep transforming to suit their unneurotic needs.

If, at this point, you wonder whether it is really possible for so many to mangle so much with so little, let me assure you that they do, they do. (See Arthur Winsome Platt's admirable study, *Humor, Dialect and Catharsis*, published by the Rutgers Press.) *

"Did your academic training help you as a writer?"

Of course. Everything helps a writer, except money and his family.

But a writer writes not because he is educated but because he is driven by the need to communicate. Behind the need to communicate is the need to share. Behind the need to share is the terrible and remorseless need to be understood.

The writer wants to be understood much more than he wants to be respected or praised or even loved. And

---

*On second thought, don't try. Professor Platt taught at Rutgers for years, but was asked to resign when they discovered he wasn't real. I just made him up to add the weight of authority to my argument. I hope this teaches you not to be impressed by footnotes.

that, perhaps, is what makes him different from others.

Writing is an internal dialogue—in which one part of the self tries to make itself understood by another. The writer's first audience is that segment of himself which listens, which judges, which contains the awful power of respite from confusion and pain. It is through what he extracts from the ferment of his own depths that the writer seeks clarity and grace. Readers, critics, brickbats, bouquets—these can only diminish or augment the resonances of debate in the auditorium within.

Every writer is a narcissist. This does not mean that he is vain; it only means that he is hopelessly self-absorbed. No one understands a writer more than he understands himself. I did not say "better"; I said "more."

It is often claimed that a writer's deepest satisfaction lies in being read. I do not think this so. His deepest satisfaction lies in the silent alchemy of writing itself. Not to be read is a painful prospect; but it is punishment deferred. The unutterable joy lies in the intense and passionate involvement of writing itself, in the stubborn exploration of the self, in that excitement and ecstasy which attend our groping among the shadows and edifices of the sunless world.

Education, a pearl beyond price, does not much help the *writing* part of a writer. Nor does scholarship. Intellectuals seem to me to place too high a premium on the sheer ingestion of data. Since they confuse obscurity with profundity, is it surprising that they mistake bibliography for brains? The tragedy of the uncreative scholar is that he has spent so many years in autopsy that his mind has become a morgue.

I, for one, think that it makes a good deal of difference *what* a man studies—whether he devotes his life to knotholes or to Plato, or wastes time that can be sanctified by Montaigne in finger exercises on Magog which impress only those whom the French, with their peerless sense of the antiseptic, call *idiots savants*.

I am of the bias that erudition is often a form of self-indulgence. It also serves as a mask for stupidity. Reading can suffocate thinking. To think *while* reading, to think about and around and beneath what one reads, is the noblest pleasure man can pursue—by himself, that is.

Were the sheer number of words that pass before the eye any index of wisdom or virtue, typesetters would be the paragons of our world.

"When will you write another book about Mr. Kaplan?"

It always saddened me to have that question asked, and I always felt guilty that I could not answer that I was in fact working on a sequel. There are many reasons why I wrote no stories about Mr. Kaplan for so long.

First, there was the War. That took a *lot* of my time.

Then, in order to feed a family all of whom had hollow legs, I wrote a good many other things—from travel sketches to melodramas to screenplays. I even wrote learned books. (*I*, at least, learned something.)

But the secret for which I searched, and which I did not find, was the "stance" from which to write. I know no better word. By "stance" I mean the position from which one views the material, from which one apprehends the characters, from which one selects the instruments of technique.

If you will compare Evelyn Waugh's " 'This is my daughter,' said the Bishop with some disgust," to Yogi Berra's acknowledgment of the praises and presents with which his fans showered him at Yankee Stadium on Yogi Berra Day ("I want to thank everyone who made this day necessary") you will see what I mean.

To those who now ask, as they may, how and why I came to write this new book about Mr. Kaplan, I can say only this:

It came about in the horrid summer of 1958, during one of the most harrowing stretches of my life, when the gods were throwing rocks at me, with a glee unworthy of them, and I wandered in the arctic reaches of solitude. Thrown upon the need for affection, and finding neither giver nor taker in the hot and beating city—so lusty, so vulgar, so various and wonderful, but not, during that nightmare, for me—I turned once more to the congregations of the self for—yes, for self-administered consolation. And, by God, it was Mr. Kaplan who appeared—his zest undiminished by the years, his spirit unvanquished, frankly annoyed by the length of time it had taken me to realize what was really important in life, willing to forgive if I would regret, spilling over with that *noblesse oblige* which my mother had taught me (whose grandfather was a philosopher and a teacher of repute) is the hallmark of the only true aristocrats in this sorry vale. Mr. Kaplan treated bygones as if they were bagels and consented to collaborate once more.

Months and months later, the sweet torments of writing having run their course, I sit here writing the words you are now reading.

In the dark colony of night, when I consider man's magnificent capacity for malice, madness, folly, envy, rage and destructiveness, and when I wonder whether we shall not all end up as breakfast for the newts and polyps, I seem to hear the muffled cries of all the words in all the books with covers closed.

As I wrote for another occasion:

Print is our passport to truth. It opens the richest empire man knows—the empire of the human heart and mind. Men die; devices change; success and fame run their course. But within the walls of even the smallest library in our land lie the treasures, the wisdom and the wonder of man's greatest adventures on this earth.

My thanks go out to all of you, unnamed but not forgotten, who made this book necessary.

LEO ROSTEN

Christmas Eve
1958

The Return of
H*Y*M*A*N K*A*P*L*A*N

"Miss Fanny Gidwitz."

"Prazent."

"Mr. Stanislaus Wilkomirski."

"I am."

"Mrs. Molly Yanoff."

"Likevise."

Mr. Parkhill tried to call the names cheerfully as he went down the roster of the beginners' grade of the American Night Preparatory School for Adults. But he did not really feel cheerful; he felt vaguely depressed.

It was only the second night of the fall term, and a new term always brought with it a fresh promise—new faces, new problems, new challenges. Yet here and now, a brief forty-eight hours after the season's advent, Mr. Parkhill found himself possessed of a strange melancholy, a nostalgia for last year's names and faces. Ah, that *had* been a beginners' grade....

"Mrs. V. Rodriguez."

"*Sí.*"

"Miss Clara Kipnis."

"Also."

"Peter Ignatius Studniczka."

"Uh."

A silly phrase kept running through Mr. Parkhill's mind: "Where are the Blooms of yesteryear?" Mr. Norman Bloom, rumor had it, had forsaken the temple of learning to toil in the vineyards of Boston for a raincoat manufacturer. (What a fierce classroom debater Mr. Bloom had been.) Promotion had advanced the more accomplished scholars—Mr. Schmitt, Miss Valuskas, Mr. Feigenbaum—to the golden reaches of Miss Higby's Composition, Grammar, and Civics. Mr. Jacob Rubin had captured the heart of a comely divorcée and had moved, it was said, to a bucolic cottage in Far Rockaway by the sea. And Mr. Hyman Kaplan...Mr. Parkhill sighed. He always sighed, automatically, when he thought of Mr. Kaplan.

"Miss Bessie Shimmelfarb."

"In place."

"Mr. Gus Matsoukas."

"Yos."

"Miss Shirley Ziev."

"Mmh."

Anyway, a good many of the veterans were back, Mr. Parkhill caught himself thinking: Miss Mitnick, a student any teacher would envy him—terribly conscientious, terribly shy, a wisp of a maiden whom only a technicality vis-à-vis attendance had denied the cherished rewards of promotion to Miss Higby's grade; Mrs. Moskowitz, as massive and doleful as ever, heaving her double chins and ample bosom in that damp despair which always accompanied her efforts to scale the heartless ramparts of English; Carmen Caravello, hot of temper, swift to take umbrage, a Latin Valkyrie; Mr. Sam Pinsky, a little more bald, a little less chubby, by trade a baker, in spirit a man fashioned by his Maker for the express purpose of playing Sancho Panza to Mr. Kaplan's Don Quixote....Mr. Pinsky was at the moment ensconced directly in front of Mr. Parkhill, in the seat in the exact center of the front row. Mr. Parkhill frowned. That had always been where Mr. Kaplan sat. (How could one forget the place from which Mr. Kaplan had once referred to the Generalissimo of Nationalist China as "Shanghai Jack"?)

Mr. Parkhill put the attendance sheet to one side. "Well, class," he addressed his flock with a reassuring smile. "Your homework for tonight, the first assignment of the semester, was—er—'My Life'." The first assignment of the year was always "My Life"; the second might be "My Vacation," or "My Job," or "My Ambition"; but the first was always "My Life." Mr. Parkhill felt that nothing so promptly enlisted the interest of his novitiates, so rapidly soothed their anxieties and bolstered their morale, as the invitation to recount the story of their lives.

"Mrs. Tomasic, will you please write your composition on the board?...Mr. Matsoukas...Miss Tarnova...."

They trudged to the front of the room in the single file of the doomed, seven of them: one groaned, two sagged, three sighed, one shuddered. But all advanced to meet their fate. They strung themselves along the blackboard as if deploying for battle. Brows furrowed, lips tightened, papers rustled—then sticks of chalk were raised like lances. A few coughs of apology, a few moans of anguish, and white letters began to form words that marched bravely across the ominous slate.

Mr. Parkhill strolled down the aisle to the back of the room, where he turned to watch them.

Tiny Mrs. Tomasic was standing on tiptoe as she committed her homework to the board with birdlike scratchings. Miss Pomeranz kept wiping her lips with her handkerchief as concentration exacted its toll. Mr. Matsoukas muttered. (Every class Mr. Parkhill had ever had seemed to contain one born mutterer: Gus Matsoukas, who sought no friends and tendered no confidences, as befitted a Greek among barbarians, was the mutterer of the beginners' grade.) Mr. Oscar Trabish unbuttoned his collar to restore the circulation in his writing arm. Mr. Plonsky, who was both farsighted and nearsighted, kept adjusting his bifocals —the better to stare at his work or glare at Miss Tarnova, on his right. Miss Tarnova, a buxom ex-ballerina with raven hair and innumerable bracelets which jangled as she wrote, relapsed into throaty breathings whenever she lifted chalk or pen. (She was a sort of faded Cleopatra, floating down a Slavic Nile, lost in dreams of the days when men, maddened by her beauty, had drunk champagne out of her slipper.) Neither the tinkle of her gewgaws nor the ire of Reuben Plonsky could disturb the haze of romance which enveloped Olga Tarnova at the board. She raised a perfumed handkerchief to her nostrils and sniffed.

Mr. Parkhill noticed how silence had fallen upon the seated. The tick of the big clock on the wall, stern Washington on one side, sad Lincoln on the other, now punctuated the air. And once more memory stirred in Mr. Parkhill. In *last* year's class, he could not help ruminating, harbingers of excitement would long since have appeared—from Mr. Bloom, as he pounced upon some blunder just hatched on the board; or from Miss Valuskas, whose Finnish pencil used to stab upward at the first sign of error; or from Mr. Kaplan, as he "t'ought" about some profound grammatical point. (Mr. Kaplan had always thought out loud—either to consult some private muse, of whom he had a copious supply, or to give his colleagues the pleasure of participating in the secrets of his singular dialectic. On one wild, memorable night, Mr. Kaplan had recited the principal parts of "to eat" as "eat, ate, full." On another, he had given the opposite of "inhale" as "dead.") Nostalgia descended on Mr. Parkhill like a shroud.

He started to open the window, for no good reason, when, quite without warning, the door was flung open. A gust of cold air swept in from the corridor as a clarion voice proclaimed, "Hollo, frands, students, averybody! Grittings!" The heads of the thirty-odd pilgrims in the classroom turned as one. "Valcome to de new sizzon! Valcome to beginnis' grate!"

"Mine gootness!" exclaimed Mrs. Moskowitz. "I dun't believe mine ice!"

"Lookit, lookit who's here na!" rejoiced Mr. Pinsky.

"Holy smoky," someone growled.

Miss Caravello murmured something with "Santa Maria" in it. It might have been a prayer.

Mr. Parkhill did not have to turn to recognize the heroic voice that had cried "Grittings!" He could not mistake that incomparable enunciation, that supreme aplomb, that blithe, triumphant spirit. He knew only one student who would cry "Valcome!" to those who, enjoying prior residence, should clearly have welcomed *him*. He knew only one man who entered a classroom as if storming a citadel. "Mr.—" his eyes found the ebullient newcomer—"Kaplan. Well, well, Mr. Kaplan!"

It *was* Mr. Kaplan, proud, undaunted, a knight returned to the lists of glory. He looked a bit more debonair, a trifle more euphoric. His face was deeply sunburned, which so accented the natural luminosity of his features that a bright light seemed to be shining under his skin. And he was freckled! How odd. Mr. Kaplan, the very apostle and epitome of urban civilization, freckled. For one absurd moment, Mr. Parkhill had the notion that the freckles were shaped like stars, so that Mr. Kaplan's countenance echoed his name as he always wrote it—the letters in red crayon, outlined in blue, the stars green: H*Y*M*A*N K*A*P*L*A*N. Mr. Parkhill even wondered how the freckles would look in red and blue and green. He repressed this foolish fantasy, severely.

"Hollo, Mr. Pockheel! Harre you?" Mr. Kaplan was exclaiming. "Oh, I'm so heppy to seeink you I ken't tell abot." Mr. Parkhill found himself shaking Mr. Kaplan's hand numbly. "You lookink fine! Foistcless! *A* Number Vun!"

"You—er—look fine yourself," said Mr. Parkhill cautiously. "Just splendid."

"Denk you," said Mr. Kaplan, with a certain elegance. "It's nice you should say."

"I—I'm glad to see you back, Mr. Kaplan."

"I'm besite you mit joy!"

Mr. Parkhill started to say "It's 'I'm beside *myself*,' Mr. Kaplan," but it was too late. Mr. Kaplan had turned to the class with a gesture that combined the gracious and the magisterial, and declaimed: "Fallow-students in beginnis' grate, ve vill voik togadder! Ve vill slafe! Ve vill *loin*!" He raised an imperial finger to the sky. "Vun for all an' all for Mr. Pockheel!"

"Walcome home, Mr. Napoleon," said Mr. Blattberg morosely, touching his gold chain, from which two baby teeth dangled, as if it were an amulet.

Mr. Kaplan's gaze passed across subversive Blattberg coolly. ("*Elephantus non capit murem*," Mr. Parkhill thought, promptly chiding himself for the outlandish image of elephants not bothering to capture mice.) "Aha! Mitnick."

Miss Mitnick, a fawn flushed out of her thicket, turned a rosy hue and stammered, "Hello, Mr. Kaplan."

"So you beck, too," he sighed. "Hau Kay." He said it as if approving her credentials. "I soggest—"

"Take a seat, Mr. Kaplan," said Mr. Parkhill hastily.

Mr. Kaplan nodded (it was a nod of collaboration) and stepped to the seat in the center of the front row. "Pinsky."

Mr. Pinsky beamed. "Keplen."

"Podden me. You got mine sitt." Mr. Kaplan said it simply, without the slightest tinge of displeasure, a sovereign returned to reclaim his throne.

At once Mr. Pinsky gathered up books and papers and slid into the seat beyond. He appeared delighted to surrender the hallowed place. He had, indeed, never thought of himself as other than Mr. Kaplan's shield bearer, holding the keep against upstarts until his lord returned from some crusade.

"Who *is* Mr. Koplen?" whispered Hans Guttman. (Mr. Guttman was a raw recruit to the ranks.)

"You'll see," was all that Mr. Plonsky, who could barely see, replied moodily.

"Now, class…" Mr. Parkhill called.

The students at the board were so beguiled by the

fanfare that had attended Hyman Kaplan's entrance and investiture that they had forgotten all about their autobiographies. They were too busy giving the prodigal son ripe smiles, if friend, or wary salutations, if foe. Those who were neither friend nor foe, like Mr. Scymzak, looked bewildered: only a fool could deny that neutrality faced grave crises in the hours ahead.

"Come, come, class," called Mr. Parkhill. "Let us get back to our work. Mr. Kaplan will be with us for quite a while."

"Alvays," murmured Mr. Kaplan.

A picture of Mr. Kaplan in the front row, timeless, unchanged and unchangeable, swam before Mr. Park-hill's eyes. He winced.

The seven at the board returned to their labors. Mr. Kaplan took a fountain pen out of his pocket, narrowed his eyes, scanned all the titles on the board with light-ning dispatch, cocked his head to one side, whispered "Aha! So is de homevoik abot pest livink!" and began scribbling in his notebook furiously. Mr. Parkhill wondered what on earth he had seen to make him start scribbling so furiously so *soon*.

"Let us finish, please...."

They returned from their ordeal at last, with sighs and alibis and apologies. There was merit in their unconfidence. The autobiographies of the seven con-tained some remarkable surprises.

Mrs. Tomasic, unaware of the fateful significance of the possessive adjective, had given history a brisk "Story of Life." Mr. Trabish had expatiated on "My Wife" instead of "My Life." (Mr. Parkhill discovered, to his dismay, that Mr. Trabish sometimes confused "l"s with "w"s and "w"s with "l"s.) Miss Tarnova, ever true to Mother Russia, had penned a dirge called "Life. Death. What They Mean???" Mr. Gus Matsoukas had composed a confessional which consisted of but three trenchant lines:

> Come N.Y. since 6 years.
> Work in "Acropolis—Figs & olivs."
> Marry. feel nice in morning.

And Carmen Caravello, disregarding the assignment altogether, had written a chauvinistic tribute to "Great Garibaldi."

Mr. Parkhill did not glance at the other two compositions. He felt distressed. "Let us take Mrs. Tomasic's composition first. Corrections, anyone?"

Mrs. Tomasic lowered her head; she looked like a sparrow. Her colleagues gaped at the blackboard; they looked like embalmers.

"Mistakes?" asked Mr. Parkhill lightly.

Silence.

"We need not feel so—er—shy, class. We *learn* from our mistakes....Anyone?"

No one.

Mr. Parkhill looked hopefully toward Miss Mitnick. Miss Mitnick blushed. He glanced toward Mr. Hans Guttman, the promising fledgling. Mr. Guttman was sharpening his pencil. His eye fell on Rochelle Goldberg, but Miss Goldberg was unwrapping a caramel, with which she proceeded to bolster her morale. He even gazed encouragingly at Mr. Kaplan, but Mr. Kaplan was still scribbling in that precious notebook like a man possessed, oblivious of the world.

Mr. Parkhill corrected Mrs. Tomasic's homework

himself. And he proceeded to diagnose the other autobiographies in expert, if nervous, stride. He seemed in a
hurry. Then he sent another batch of students to the
board. "Mr. Marcus...Miss Gidwitz...Peter Studniczka....'

Suddenly Mr. Kaplan's composition book began to
wave in the air like a pendulum. "Mr. Pockheel!" His
face was radiant. "Ken *I* go plizz?"

Mr. Parkhill averted his gaze. "We are doing the
*home*work, Mr. Kaplan, the work that was assigned—"

"I jost finished. In dis exect spot!"

Admiration leaped into the face of Mr. Pinsky, who
exclaimed "Pssh!" and slapped himself on the cheek in
delight.

"You—er—wrote your autobiography *here*?" Mr.
Parkhill cleared his throat.

"De whole voiks!" And with this, Mr. Kaplan leaped
from his seat to the board, seized a piece of chalk, and,
before Mr. Parkhill could either demur or dissuade,
printed in large, uncompromising letters:

Hyman Kaplan
by
H*Y*M*A*N K*A*P*L*A*N

The title plunged Mr. Parkhill into a kind of hypnotic
daze. How had Mr. Kaplan decided where to place the
stars? In the first "Hyman Kaplan"? That would imply
that it was the *idea* of Mr. Kaplan, not the real Mr.
Kaplan, that was all-important. In both "Hyman
Kaplan"s? That would suggest a split personality. But
putting the stars only in the second "Hyman Kaplan,"
as Mr. Kaplan had so masterfully decided—that

seemed incontestable: for it emphasized Kaplan the man, not Kaplan the subject, Kaplan the creator, not Kaplan the concept.

Mr. Parkhill tore his eyes from Mr. Kaplan's composition to scan the work of the others at the board. Mr. Marcus was copying an epic entitled "Who I am." Miss Kipnis was baring her soul in a saga called, rather mysteriously, "riga 19." (It turned out that "riga 19" referred to the city and date of Miss Kipnis' nativity.) Most surprising was the composition, if that was what it was, of Mr. Peter Studniczka, who had poured the story of his life into a somewhat synoptical mold:

Moth. & Fath.	Mary & Frank
broth.	6
sist.	3
	—
broth. & sist.	9
dead	2 (sist.)
Wife	No
childs	not
want be	electric work Boss

Mr. Parkhill turned his back to the board. It was easier that way. He waited for his neophytes to finish, and he heard them return to their seats, one by one. "Let us begin." He took a deep breath. "Mr. Kaplan." Only then did he turn to savor the full flowering of Mr. Kaplan's peculiar genius.

Hyman Kaplan

by

H✳Y✳M✳A✳N K✳A✳P✳L✳A✳N

> First, I was born.
> In Kiev, in old contry. (Moishe Elman, famous
> on fiddle, is also coming from Kiev.)

"Notice the sentence structure, class," said Mr. Parkhill absently; his mind was not on sentence structure at all: it was wrestling with the remorseless logic of that "First, I was born."

> My father had the name Joe but freinds
> were calling him Yussel. My mother had the
> name Ida, but I called her Mama.

"Watch for errors in—er—spelling," said Mr. Parkhill.

> Also was 4 brothers and sisters. All nice.
> Avrum, Sophie, me (my name was Hymie),
> Becky. Behind Becky came Max. Max is
> tarrible smart. He got a wonderful mamory,
> only he forgats.

"Pay attention to the *meaning* of the sentences," Mr. Parkhill announced resolutely.

> Came bad times (plenty) so I arrive in
> wonderful U.S. 10 days on ship and sick
> also 10 days. I falt sure is allready Good-
> bye, Hyman Kaplan!

"And the punctuation," admonished Mr. Parkhill.

> In N.Y. I am happy. But not 100%. So I
> am coming to school. To learn. All. I am

12

full of all kinds embition.
My mottol is—Kaplan, GO HIGH!!
T-h-e E-n-d

"The end...?" Mr. Parkhill knew it was only the beginning. He tapped his pointer on the desk firmly, to quiet the hummings and buzzings and *sotto voce* gloats that Mr. Kaplan's offerings always inspired. "Corrections?"

The gladiators leaped into the arena with zest. Mr. Blattberg denounced Mr. Kaplan for mutilating the spelling of four innocent words: "freinds...contry... mamory...embition." Mrs. Rodriguez deplored the lawlessness of Mr. Kaplan's verbs, which wandered from the present to the participial without a shred of respect for the past. Mr. Scymzak remodeled sentences with scorn and exorcised periods with contempt. Even Mrs. Yanoff, after smoothing her black dress (Mrs. Yanoff always wore black, though Mr. Yanoff was far from dead), fired scathing salvos at the solecisms Mr. Kaplan had employed and expressed heartfelt condolences for the diction he had massacred.

As Mr. Parkhill plied his chalk across the board— correcting, deleting, transposing, replacing—he could not help observing that the entire class, so placid, so subdued but half an hour ago, was agog with vitality. "Hyman Kaplan by H✳Y✳M✳A✳N K✳A✳P✳L✳A✳N" bled.

At this point Miss Mitnick mustered up enough courage to stammer, "In composition I see mistakes also in meaning." That exposed a whole new flank to the marauders.

"Procidd," Mr. Kaplan murmured, with an inscrutable smile.

"Why appears a violin player in this homework?" Miss Mitnick asked Mr. Parkhill cautiously. "Why Mr. Kaplan puts Mischa Elman in the story *his* life?"

Mr. Kaplan gazed at Miss Mitnick pityingly. "I like his playink."

"*Hanh?*" roared Mr. Plonsky in horror.

Miss Mitnick turned pale; whereupon Stanislaus Wilkomirski, a Pole known for chivalry, rushed to her defense. "No, no good!" he protested. "Is no got place, like lady says."

"*I* vant Moishe Elman should be in *mine* life," Mr. Kaplan said icily. "In *your* life put in Chopin!"

Mr. Wilkomirski fled the field with the bleat of a crushed but faithful servant.

"Stop!" cried Reuben Plonsky, riding in Wilkomirski's stead. "Objection!" He raised a challenging and insolent hand. "What kind *sanse* is in a student who writes 'Max had wonderful mamory, only he forgets'? Isn't this ridiculouse?" The ranks shook with glee. "Isn't a plain counterdiction?" The warriors formed for the charge. "Isn't like saying a man is tall but sometimes short, fat but also skinny?"

The room pealed with hilarity. Mr. Wilkomirski guffawed; Mrs. Moskowitz howled; an elfin smile even brightened Miss Mitnick's lips.

"Very good, Mr. Plonsky," said Mr. Parkhill. "There does seem to be a *contra*diction—not 'counterdiction'—in that sentence, Mr. Kaplan."

"Hoo ha," hooted Mr. Blattberg.

"You see?" grinned Cookie Kipnis. (Miss Kipnis' first name was Clara, but it pleased her no end to be called Cookie.)

14

"It's plain crazy," sneered Mr. Plonsky.

"An' vat's crazy abot?" asked Mr. Kaplan with deadly aplomb.

"How can be memory good which also isn't?" stormed Mr. Matsoukas, unable to contain himself any longer.

"Mine brodder Max has a *movvelous* mamory. But not inwincible! So occasional, he forgats."

"But Mr. Kaplan," implored Miss Mitnick, "either your brother has good memory, and remembers, or bad memory, and forgets. It *must* be one or other."

"Good fa' you!" called Miss Pomeranz.

"Ebsolutel right!" crowed Mr. Trabish.

"Mr. Koplan is caught," intoned Olga Tarnova hollowly, "tropped, tropped." (Miss Tarnova could not so much as murmur "Oxcuse" without investing it with intimations of tragedy.)

"Give Mr. Keplen a *chence*," sputtered loyal Pinsky, mopping his brow and casting yearning eyes at his liege. "His brodder is only a *human*. So maybe he—"

"No maybes!" Reuben Plonsky, implacable, thundered. "Must be one or the odder! Good mamory or bad!"

"Mr. Kaplan, give an *inch*," Bessie Shimmelfarb pleaded.

Through all this broil and brabble, Mr. Kaplan had sat silent, his eyes half closed, pondering the folly of man. Not until Miss Mitnick, under the banner of mercy, pleaded, "Admit, Mr. Kaplan. Is not so terrible to make a mistake!" did Hyman Kaplan deign to respond.

"Mine dear Mitnick," he murmured, his manner careless, his eyes still dreamy, "I regrat your pars of rizzoning. *Is* a mamory eider good or bed? A day is eider

15

hot or cold? A woman is eider beauriful or a mass? Is life so tsimple, Mitnick?" His eyes, wide open now, flashed at Reuben Plonsky. "Is man so cotton dry?"

" 'Cut-and-*dried*,' Mr. Kaplan," but Mr. Parkhill's acolyte heard him not.

"Is averyting on oit black and vhite, no inbetvinn? Ha! Rich or poor—no meedle cless? Anodder 'Ha'! Batter *t'ink* abot it, Plonsky. T'ink dipper, Mitnick!" Mr. Kaplan illustrated how to "t'ink dipper" by narrowing only one eye whilst gazing fiercely at his inquisitors with the other. "Mine brodder Max remambered a *lot*! An' vat he remambered he remambered fine! So he *did* had a fine mamory, no? Hau Kay. But *somtimes*, netcheral, it could heppen Max forgot. So does dis minn he *didn't* had a good mamory *ven ve jost agreet he did*?"

Mr. Plonsky put his head between his hands, groaning. Miss Tarnova turned beige. Miss Mitnick bit her lip. Poor Miss Mitnick: always right, but never victorious.

"No, no, *no*, Mr. Kaplan," exclaimed Mr. Parkhill reprovingly. "You have *not* met Mr. Plonsky's objection!" He plunged into the discussion with uncommon force. He could not let Mr. Kaplan carry the day with such outrageous sophistry. He would not let reason be confounded by pettifoggery. He saw his bravest, brightest scholars—Miss Mitnick, Mr. Plonsky—caught like flies in the trap of Mr. Kaplan's logic. "Mr. Kaplan, 'Max had a wonderful memory, only he forgets' is *not* acceptable," declared Mr. Parkhill frostily. "It is, in fact, self-contradictory!" He broke Mr. Kaplan's argument into its separate and deceptive postulates. He segregated premise from conclusion. He exposed the *a priori* and deposed the *non sequitur*. For this time, at the very beginning of the term's voyage, he was determined that Mr. Kaplan for once concede flagrant error.

Yet even as he chastised his most ambitious, but undisciplined, pupil, Mr. Parkhill felt the warm and nourishing juices flow once more. For the spark of life, the nerve of conflict, had been restored to what, but a few moments ago, had been a listless classroom. As he doggedly exposed each cunning nuance of the casuistry with which Mr. Kaplan had demolished his enemies, Mr. Parkhill caught himself feeling strangely grateful. Hyman Kaplan—nay, H*Y*M*A*N K*A*P*L*A*N! —had returned.

Christopher K*A*P*L*A*N

To Mr. Parkhill the beginners' grade was more than a congregation of students yearning to master English. He took a larger view of his responsibilities: to Mr. Parkhill the American Night Preparatory School for Adults was an incubator of Citizens. To imbue the men and women of a dozen nations with the meaning of America—its past, its traditions, its aspirations—this, to Mr. Parkhill, was the greater work to which he had dedicated himself.

So it was that on the eve of any national holiday, Mr. Parkhill devoted at least half an hour to a little excursion into our history. In the spring, it was Decoration Day that enlisted his eloquence. In the fall it was Armistice Day and Thanksgiving. (He always regretted the fact that the Fourth, grandest holiday of them all, fell in a month when the school was not in session.) And this Monday night in October, on the eve of Columbus Day, Mr. Parkhill opened the class with these ringing words: "Tonight, let us set aside our routine tasks for a while to consider the man whose—er—historic achievement the world will commemorate tomorrow."

Expectancy murmured its sibilant path across the room.

"To this man," Mr. Parkhill continued, "the United States—America—owes its very beginning. I'm sure you all know whom I mean, for he—"

"Jawdge Vashington!" Miss Fanny Gidwitz promptly guessed.

"No, no. Not *George W*ashington—watch that 'w,' Miss Gidwitz. I refer to—'

"Paul Rewere!" cried Oscar Trabish impetuously.

Mr. Parkhill adjusted his spectacles. Mr. Trabish had formed some peculiar psychic union with "Paul Rewere": he had already written two rhapsodic compositions and made one fiery speech on his beloved alter ego. (The compositions had been called "Paul Revere's Horse Makes History" and "Paul Revere. One by Land, Two by the Beach." The speech had been announced by Mr. Trabish as "Paul Rewere! Vhy He Vasn't Prazidant?" He had been quite indignant about it.)

Mr. Parkhill shook his head. "Not Paul '*Rewere*.' It's a 'v,' Mr. Trabish, not a 'w.' You spell it correctly when you write, but you seem to replace the 'v's with 'w's— and the 'w's with 'v's—when you speak. Class, let's not guess. What *date* is tomorrow?"

"Mine boitday!" an excited voice sang out.

Mr. Parkhill ignored that. "Tomorrow," he said firmly, "is October twelfth. And on October twelfth, 1492—" He got no further.

"Dat's mine *boit*day! October tvalf! I should live so! Honist!" It was (but why, oh why, did it have to be?) the proud, enraptured voice of Hyman Kaplan.

Mr. Parkhill took a deep breath, a slow, deep breath, and said cautiously, "Mr. Kaplan, is October twelfth— er—really your birthday?"

Mr. Kaplan's eyes widened—innocent, hurt. "*Mister*

20

Pockheel!"

Mr. Parkhill felt ashamed of himself.

Stanislaus Wilkomirski growled, "Kaplan too old for have birtday."

"October tvalf I'm born; October tvalf I'm tsalebratink!" Mr. Kaplan retorted. "All mine *life* I'm hevink boitdays October tvalf. No axceptions!"

Mr. Parkhill said, "Well, well, well. That *is* a coincidence. October twelfth. Hmmm." He cleared his throat uneasily. "I'm sure we all wish Mr. Kaplan many happy returns."

Mr. Kaplan beamed, rose, bowed, beamed, and sat down, beaming.

Miss Mitnick, feeling the occasion called for good will and peace among men, stammered, "Congratulation." (Habit, not intention, accounted for the singular.)

"Denks," said Mr. Kaplan, all *savoir faire*.

"However," Mr. Parkhill raised his voice, "the particular historical event we are commemorating tomorrow pertains to—Christopher Columbus. For it was on October twelfth, 1492—"

"Co*lom*biss!" Mr. Kaplan's rapture passed beyond containment. "Christover Co*lom*biss?!"

Excitement seized the beginners' grade.

"Columbus!"

"Columbia Day," breathed Olga Tarnova. "Romahnteek."

"Colombos discovert America!"

"Oy!" That was Mrs. Moskowitz. No one could groan a "What?" or moan a "Why?" with one-tenth the eloquence Sadie Moskowitz put into her "Oy!" She was the Niobe of the beginners' grade.

"Yes, class, on October twelfth, 1492—"

Mr. Trabish dropped a sneer in the general direction of Fanny Gidwitz. "And you said Jawdge Vashington!"

"*You* said Paul Rewere!"

"On October twelfth, 1492—" Mr. Parkhill persevered.

"By me could avery day in year be somthing about Paul Rewere!" proclaimed Oscar Trabish.

"And by *me* is our foist Prazident vert ten hossriders!" scowled Fanny Gidwitz.

Miss Goldberg reached for a nougat.

"*On October twelfth, 1492—*" Mr. Parkhill's voice rose until it brooked no ignoring— "Christopher Columbus discovered a new continent!"

The class simmered down at last, and Mr. Parkhill launched upon the deathless saga of Christopher Columbus and the brave little armada that sailed into the unknown. He spoke slowly, impressively, almost with fervor. (It was not often he was afforded material of such majesty and such momentousness.) And the thirty-odd novitiates of the beginners' grade, caught up in the drama of that great and fearful voyage, hung upon each word. "The food ran low. Water was scarce. Rumors of doom—of disaster—raced through the sailors' ranks...."

Goldie Pomeranz leaned forward and sighed moistly into Mr. Kaplan's ear, "You soitinly locky, Mr. Kaplan. Born same day Columbus did."

Mr. Kaplan was in a world of dreams. He kept whispering to himself, "Christover Colombiss," the name a talisman. "My!" He closed his eyes to be alone with his hero. "October tvalf I'm arrivink in de void, an' October tvalf Colombiss picks ot for discoverink U.S.!

Dastiny!"

"Mutiny faced Christopher Columbus," said Mr. Parkhill with feeling.

"My boitday is Motch toity," Miss Pomeranz confided to Mr. Kaplan in a sadness fraught with envy. (Miss Pomeranz was a fitter in a shop that specialized in "bridal gons.") "Not even a *soborb* vas discovered Motch toity."

Mr. Kaplan gave Miss Pomeranz a glance both modest and consoling. "Ufcawss, Colombiss discovert lonk bifore Keplen arrived."

"October twalf is October twalf!" cried Mr. Pinsky, his equerry.

Mr. Kaplan allowed the mantle of history to fall upon his shoulders.

Mr. Parkhill, upon whom the Pomeranz-Kaplan-Pinsky symposium was not lost, described the geographical outposts of 1492, the innocent belief that the world was flat as a plate, the mockery to which Columbus had been subjected. He traced the ironic confluence of events through which the new continent had been named after Amerigo Vespucci.

"By *mistake?*" Mr. Kaplan asked incredulously, and at once replied "By mistake!" in indignation.

Mr. Parkhill recounted the course of that immortal voyage, three tiny ships on an ocean infested, in men's minds, by demons of the deep. He sketched the iron resolve of the captain who would not turn back. When he said, "And then a voice from the crow's-nest cried 'Land! Land!'" a tear crept into Miss Mitnick's eye. When he described the landing on new soil, Miss Tarnova suppressed a sob. And when he said, "And because Columbus thought he was really in India, he

23

called the natives Indians," the amazement of his flock burst its bonds.

"Vun mistake on top de odder!" cried Mr. Kaplan.

"Dey called Hindyans by *mistake*?" moaned Mrs. Moskowitz. Mrs. Moskowitz could not believe that of history.

"Yes, Mrs. Moskowitz, by mistake," said Mr. Parkhill.

Mr. Kaplan shook his head three times. "Dose poor Indians."

Mrs. Tomasic fingered her crucifix.

Mr. Parkhill hurried on to the role of Ferdinand and Isabella. Just before he completed the absorbing tale, Mr. Kaplan announced, "Ectual, ve ain't Amaricans!"

Mr. Parkhill paused, " 'Actual*ly*,' we '*are*n't' Americans, Mr. Kaplan. There is no such word as—"

"Ectual, ve all Colombians!" Mr. Kaplan exclaimed. A demand for justice—however long overdue—burned in his eyes.

Mr. Parkhill turned the class over to Miss Mitnick for General Discussion. General Discussion, Mr. Parkhill had found, was a most fruitful exercise, particularly when he invited one of the more competent students to lead it. General Discussion was even more productive than Recitation and Speech: it roused fewer anxieties in the breasts of the timid; it spread the burdens of participation.

Miss Mitnick struck the keynote for the evening with a touching, if embarrassed, eulogy of explorers in general and Columbus in particular. She ended her tribute with a deft comparison of Columbus and Admiral Byrd. "Both men fond new places for humanity. Natchelly, in different places."

"Edmiral Boyd?" Mr. Kaplan promptly sniffed in disdain. It was clear that henceforth anyone drawing comparisons between Christopher Columbus and lesser spirits would have to answer to Hyman Kaplan. "Vat kine finder new tings vas dis Edmiral Boyd?"

"It's '*Ad*miral *By*rd,'" Mr. Parkhill suggested from the seat he had taken in the back of the room.

"Admiral Byrd was a kind *modern* Columbus," Miss Mitnick said nervously.

"Vat he discovert could compare mit Columbiss's vundefful didd?" Mr. Kaplan demanded.

"Admiral Byrd discovered Sout Pole!"

"Som discoverink!" said Mr. Kaplan, dismissing all of Antarctica.

"Stop!" roared Mr. Plonsky, his glare thrice magnified by his lenses. "South Pole is important as North, maybe more."

"Ha!" parried Mr. Kaplan. "Averybody *knew* vas a Sot Pole, no? All Edmiral Boyd did vas go dere!"

Miss Mitnick turned white. Mr. Plonsky was so infuriated that he turned his back on Mr. Kaplan and, facing the rear wall, appealed to the gods: "Crazy! Cuckoo! How you can argue with a Mr. Opside Don?"

"Admiral Byrd is big *hero*," Miss Mitnick faltered, wetting her lips. "He went through terrible things for humanity—cold, icebergs, alone, freezings."

"Edmiral Boyd *vent mit all modinn conweniences*!" ruled Hyman Kaplan.

Miss Mitnick made a strangling sound and shot an S.O.S. to Mr. Parkhill.

"Er—it's '*Ad*miral *Byrd*,'" Mr. Parkhill repeated. Nobody paid any attention to him. For Miss Caravello, a never-dormant volcano, had erupted: "Is only da one

Columbus! No more lak—before, behinda!" To Miss Caravello, beyond any peradventure of doubt, Columbus would forever be enshrined as a peculiarly Italian phenomenon, unparalleled, incomparable. Admiral Byrd, she said flatly, was a "copying cat." For great Columbus, Miss Caravello concluded hotly, nothing short of a thousand "Bravo"s would do. She proceeded to give three of them: "Bravo! Bravo! Bravo!"

The Messrs. Kaplan and Pinsky broke into applause.

"Class—"

Now Mr. Gus Matsoukas demanded the floor, and took it before Miss Mitnick could recognize him. "Colomb' good man, no doubts about," he began magnanimously. Columbus was, indeed, worth all that Mr. Kaplan and Miss Caravello had claimed for him. But after all, Mr. Matsoukas insinuated, how could any but the uncultivated regard Columbus as more than a dull descendant of the first and *greatest* explorer— Ulysses? (Ulysses, it turned out, was born no more than seventeen kilometers from Mr. Matsoukas' birthplace.)

"Boit*days* are more important den boitplaces!" Mr. Kaplan proclaimed.

Mr. Matsoukas, startled, could think of no rejoinder to this powerful and unexpected postulate. He retired, mumbling.

"Anybody else wants to say few words?" asked Miss Mitnick anxiously.

Mr. Kaplan thrust his hand into the air.

"Floor is ebsolutely *open*," Miss Mitnick announced, keeping her eyes where Mr. Kaplan's could not meet them. "*Any*body can talk."

Mr. Kaplan promptly rose, said, "Foidinand an' Isabel. Ha!" and sat down.

Uneasy murmurs raced across the room. Miss Mitnick flushed and twisted her handkerchief around her fingers. "Mr. Kaplan," she stammered, "I didn't catch."

Mr. Kaplan got up again, repeated, "Foidinand an' Isabel. Ha!" and again sat down.

"Why he is anger?" whispered Mrs. Tomasic.

"He is mod, mod," groaned Olga Tarnova.

"Er—Mr. Kaplan," Mr. Parkhill began, "I do think—"

"Axplain!" Mr. Blattberg sang out. "Describe!" (It was through such clarity and persistence that Aaron Blattberg had become one of the best shoe salesmen on Second Avenue.)

Mr. Kaplan snorted, but said nothing.

"Keplan wants to talk or Keplan *not* wants to talk?" Mr. Plonsky inquired of the rear wall bitterly.

"Y-yes, Mr. Kaplan," Mr. Parkhill frowned, "I do think the class is entitled to some explanation of your—er—comment."

"All of a sodden Mr. Keplen makes fun Foidinand Isabel!" protested Mrs. Moskowitz. "Not even saying 'Axcuse' can he make 'Ha, ha!' on kinks and quinns?!"

This frontal attack stirred the royalties into action.

"Talk, Kaplan?"

"You got the floor, no?"

"Tell awreddy!"

A more formal dialectician cried, "Give your meanink dose remocks!" That was Mrs. Yanoff, an epistemologist in black.

Mr. Kaplan rose once more and turned to face his challengers. "Ladies an' gantlemen, Mr. Pockheel—an' chairlady." Miss Mitnick lowered her eyes. "Ve all agreeink Colombiss's joiney vas vun de most movellous tings aver heppened in de voild." Cries, calls, grunts of

27

affirmation. "*T'ink* abot det treep, jost *t'ink*. Viks an' viks Colombiss vas sailink—tru storm, lighteninks, tonder. Tru vafes high like Ampire State Buildink. Fodder an' fodder Colombiss vent—alone!" Mr. Kaplan paused to let the awesome data of that ordeal sink home. "Vell, mine frands, in *vat kine boats* Colombiss made det vunderful voyitch?" Mr. Kaplan's eyes narrowed. "In fency sheeps? In fine accommodations? No! In leetle, teentsy chizz boxes! Boats full likks! Boats full doit, joims, vater commink in! *Som* boats for discoverink Amarica! An' det's vy I'm sayink, '*Shame* on you, Foidinand! *Shame* on you, Isabel!'" Mr. Kaplan's eyes flashed. "Couldn't dey give a man like Colombiss batter transportation?"

Outrage exploded in the classroom.

"*Viva* Columbus!" cried Mrs. Rodriguez, upon whom it had just dawned that Columbus owed much to Iberia.

"Crazy talk," muttered Mr. Matsoukas, thinking of the raft of Ulysses.

"Maybe in 1492 they should manufacture already a S.S. *Qvinn Lizabeth*?" Mr. Plonsky asked the rear wall sarcastically.

A storm of retorts, defenses, taunts, disclaimers filled the air. Miss Mitnick, staggering under the responsibilities of arbitration, kept pleading, "Mr. Kaplan, please, Mr. Kaplan." Her cheeks kept changing from the flushed to the ashen. "Mr. Kaplan, *please*. The ships Ferdinand and Isabella gave—they were fine for that *time*."

"For de *time*? But not for de *man*!" thundered Hyman Kaplan.

"But in those days —"

"A man like Colombiss should have averyting fromm

28

de bast!"

"Oh migott," roared Mr. Plonsky.

"Kaplen, give an inch," pleaded Bessie Shimmel-farb.

Miss Tarnova moaned, "Mr. Koplan is no gantle-mon."

Mr. Parkhill got up. It seemed to be the only thing to do. "Well, class, I think—"

"Colombiss desoived more den a *Senta Maria*, a *Nina*, an' a *Pintele*!" Mr. Kaplan plunged on in his passion, hacking left and right without mercy in the service of his historical partner. "Ven a man stotts ot to discover Amarica—"

"Columbus didn't go to discover a spacific *place*," Miss Mitnick protested.

"Vat did he go for—axercise?" demanded Hyman Kaplan.

"I mean Columbus didn't *know* was America," she said in desperation. "He didn't know was a continent in middle Atlentic Ocean. Columbus just went *out*…"

Mr. Kaplan bestowed upon Miss Mitnick a look of pity laced with scorn. "He 'jost vent ot'? *Vy* he vent ot?"

"To—to discover," Miss Mitnick said tearfully.

"*Vat* to discover?"

Miss Mitnick bit her lip. "Just—to *discover*."

Mr. Kaplan surveyed the ranks of his colleagues, nodding. "Colombiss vent 'jost to discover,'" he repeated softly. "'*Jost* to discover.'" He glanced toward heaven, mourning man's naïveté. Then, his face a cloud, he struck. "Som pipple t'ink dat if a man goes ot to mail a latter he only *hopes* maybe he'll find a mail-box!"

"Stop!" howled Mr. Plonsky, smiting his forehead.

And now the battle raged once more—with shouts and cries and accusations; with righteous assaults on the Kaplan logic, and impassioned defenses of the Mitnick virtue. Mr. Plonsky bellowed that Mr. Kaplan had pulled an unfair rabbit out of an illegal hat; Mr. Pinsky retorted that Mr. Plonsky was too muddle-headed to follow the matchless precision of Mr. Kaplan's reasoning. Mrs. Yanoff charged that Mr. Pinsky was nothing but a Kaplan coolie; Miss Gidwitz rejoined that Mrs. Yanoff was but a myrmidon of Mitnick. Mr. Blattberg warned one and all that Mr. Kaplan could drive normal minds crazy; Mr. Pinsky opined that Mr. Blattberg's mental condition predated exposure to a man of Mr. Kaplan's stature. In a spate of rear-guard scuffles on the sidelines, Mr. Wilkomirski raged, Mr. Matsoukas ranted, and Mrs. Moskowitz—abandoned, forlorn—wailed in her Laodicean twilight.

"*Class*," Mr. Parkhill kept pleading, "*class*!"

In the corridors, the bell rang—but no one heard it. The bell rang again, loud and long—but no one cared.

Mr. Parkhill called, "That will be all for tonight, class." He said it automatically, but he had a worried look. For Mr. Parkhill could not help feeling that General Discussion had not been a complete success this evening. If only Columbus had discovered America on October *eleventh*; if only Hyman Kaplan had been born on October thirteenth...

The Distressing Dream of Mr. Parkhill

It was a fine evening. The moon was washing the city with silver. Mr. Parkhill looked at his watch. Forty minutes before he was due to meet his class. He decided to walk.

At this very moment, he reflected, from a dozen diverse outposts of this vast and clamorous city, his students, too, were wending their way to the American Night Preparatory School for Adults. Miss Mitnick was probably subjecting her homework to yet another revision on the Fourteenth Street bus. (What a salutary student Miss Mitnick was.) Peter Studniczka was no doubt mumbling over his battered copy of 1,000 *Words Commonly Mispelled* on the BMT express. (Sometimes Mr. Parkhill wondered whether Mr. Studniczka was as much influenced by the columns in which the words were spelled right as he seemed to be by the columns in which the words were spelled wrong.) Miss Olga Tarnova was probably conjuring up Open Questions on the Lexington subway as she brushed her excessively long eyelashes with mascara. (Mr. Parkhill often wished that Miss Tarnova, who worked for a milliner in Greenwich Village, would pay as much attention to her conjugations as she did to her cosmetics.)

31

What interesting, what *unusual* persons his students were. They came from a score of lands and cultures. He had spent almost twelve years now in the American Night Preparatory School for Adults. Twelve years ....Why, over three hundred students must have passed under his tutelage during all that time. Some he remembered quite vividly, others scarcely at all. Some had been swift to learn, others deplorably obtuse. Some were B.K. and some were A.K....Mr. Parkhill frowned. His lips drew tight in a reflex of self-chastisement. Why on *earth* was he falling into that exasperating conceit again? It was absurd, perfectly absurd. Why, then, could he not shake it off, once and for all? *Qui docet* should *discet*.

It had begun almost two weeks ago, when he had awakened with a frightful pounding of the heart, unaccountably short of breath and perspiring, from a dream—a dream that had recurred, to his dismay, again and again. There was nothing especially complicated about the dream; it contained no recondite symbols such as, Mr. Parkhill knew from rereading Freud, characterize the dreams of many men; and it surely contained nothing which could by the most fanciful stretch of the imagination be called "libidinal." No. It was just a plain, run-of-the-mill dream. This was its content:

A great crowd was gathered before the school, which was freshly painted, glistening with a strange radiance and bedecked with countless flags and gay banners. Some sort of ceremony was taking place. In one version of the dream, Mr. Leland Robinson, principal of the ANPSA, was addressing the throng; in others, the Chief Justice, in wig and black gown, was delivering the oration; and several times it had been none other than the Secretary-General of the United Nations himself who held the crowd spellbound. But it was not that part of the dream that always tore Mr. Parkhill's sleep asunder. The portion from which Mr. Parkhill awakened, his throat parched and his forehead damp, the only part of the dream, indeed, that repeated itself in identical form no matter *who* was delivering the main oration, came when the festivities suddenly stopped, a terrible hush fell upon the multitude, and Mr. Parkhill found himself the target of all eyes. They were glaring at him in peculiar accusation, as (for reasons he could never make out) he began to mount a gigantic ladder, in excruciating slow motion, with a bronze plaque strapped to his back. The ladder seemed a hundred stories high, even though it rested just above the entrance to the school. What Mr. Parkhill seemed driven to do, from that awful ladder, was hang the bronze plaque above the doorway. Engraved on the plaque in great Gothic letters was this legend:

𝔄merican 𝔑ight 𝔓reparatory 𝔖chool 𝔉or 𝔄dults

Founded 1910
b. 25 years B.K.
d. "?" years A.K.

That "?" always blazed like a neon sign, the ? in bright red and the " " in blue. The "A.K.," however, was outlined in green.

A horn howling into his very eardrum caused Mr. Parkhill to jump back to the curb just as a truck whooshed by his nose. He heard a hoarse voice implore the deity to strike him dead. Mr. Parkhill apologized to the vacant air. The traffic light was indubitably red. He had not noticed it. Or had he mistaken the red of the light for the red of the "?"? He felt ashamed of himself. He waited for the light to change—to green, of course —and hastened across the street.

"B.K."…"A.K." Oh, he knew what those cryptic notations signified. They stood for "Before Kaplan" and "After Kaplan." In fact, that was the key to the whole dream. It simply raised, in symbolic form, a thought that must be churning and churning, unresolved, through Mr. Parkhill's unconsciousness: *viz.*, that the American Night Preparatory School for Adults, which actually *had* been founded a good many years before Mr. Kaplan ever entered its doors, was doomed to survive only "?" years after Mr. Kaplan left. Left? That was just the point. Would Mr. Kaplan ever leave?

The question had haunted Mr. Parkhill long, long before he had ever had that distressing dream. For he did not see how he could, in conscience, promote Mr. Kaplan to Miss Higby's grade (only last week Mr. Kaplan had referred to the codifier of the laws of gravity as "Isaac Newman"), and he knew that he could not bring himself to advise Mr. Kaplan, as he was often tempted, to transfer to some other night school where he might perhaps be happier. The undeniable fact was that there was no other night school in which Hyman Kaplan could possibly be happier: Mr. Parkhill might be happier; Miss Higby might be happier; a dozen members of the beginners' grade would surely be happier. But Mr. Kaplan? That intrepid scholar displayed the strongest conceivable affection, an affection bordering on the lyrical, for his alma mater.

That was another thing. Strictly speaking, of course,

the ANPSA could not possibly be the alma mater of someone who had never been graduated from it; but Mr. Kaplan had a way of acting as if it were.

That was yet another of the baffling characteristics that made Mr. Kaplan so difficult to contend with: his cavalier attitude to reality, which he seemed to think he could alter to suit himself. How else could one describe a man who identified the immortal Strauss waltz as "the Blue Daniel"? Or who, in recounting the tale of the cloak spread in the mud before Queen Elizabeth, insisted on crediting the gallantry to "Sir Walter Reilly"? Or who identified our first First Lady as "Mother Washington"? True, George Washington was the father of our country, but that did not make Martha the *mother*. It was all terribly frustrating.

Every way Mr. Parkhill turned, he seemed to sink deeper and deeper into the Kaplan morass. If Mr. Kaplan could not be promoted, much less graduated, what *could* be done about him? Sometimes it looked to Mr. Parkhill as if Mr. Kaplan was deliberately trying to stay in the beginners' grade for the rest of his (i.e. Mr. Parkhill's) life. This thought had begun to bother Mr. Parkhill so much that he brought it up at the last faculty meeting.

Right after Miss Schnepfe had reminded the staff to deposit their attendance reports in her office at the end of each week, Mr. Robinson asked if there were any other problems which ought to be brought to his attention. Mr. Parkhill had cleared his throat. "What is the school's policy," he inquired, "toward a student who may *never* pass the final examination in—er—one of the lower grades?" He would not soon forget the cold, granitelike mask into which Mr. Robinson's features had composed themselves. (Few knew that under Mr. Robinson's stern exterior seethed emotions that led men to end up as what Mr. Kaplan had once called "a nervous rag.")

That left Mr. Parkhill exactly where he had been before. What could be done about Hyman Kaplan? The man simply refused to learn. No, Mr. Parkhill promptly corrected himself: It was not that Mr. Kaplan refused to learn; what Mr. Kaplan refused to do was *conform*. That was an entirely different matter. Mr. Parkhill could get Mr. Kaplan to understand a rule—about spelling or diction or punctuation; what he did not seem able to do was get Mr. Kaplan to agree with it. (Modern cities, Mr. Kaplan averred, consist of streets, boulevards, and revenues.)

Nor was that all. The laws of English, after all, have developed century after century, like the common law; and like the common law, they augment their authority precisely from the fact that men go on observing them, century after century. But Mr. Kaplan was not in the slightest impressed by precedent. He seemed to take the position that each rule of grammar, each canon of syntax, each convention of usage, no matter how ancient or how formidable, had to prove its case anew— to him. He seemed to make the whole English language start from scratch. (The plural of "sandwich," he had once declaimed, is "delicatessen.") Somewhere, somehow, Mr. Kaplan had gotten it into his head that to bend the knee to custom was but a hair's breadth from bending the neck to slavery.

And there was another perplexity. Whereas all the other students came to school in order to be instructed, Mr. Kaplan seemed to come in order to be consulted. It had taken a good deal of persuasion on Mr. Parkhill's part, for instance, to convince Mr. Kaplan that there simply is no feminine form of "ghost." If the feminine of "host" is "hostess," Mr. Kaplan had observed, then surely the feminine of "ghost" should be "ghostess."

It was most trying. Not that Mr. Kaplan was an obstreperous student. On the contrary. Not one of Mr. Parkhill's three hundred abecedarians had ever been more eager, more enthusiastic, more athirst and aflame for knowledge. The trouble was that Mr. Kaplan was so eager, so enthusiastic, so athirst and aflame that he managed to convert the classroom into a courtroom—a courtroom, moreover, in which the entire English language found itself put on the stand as defendant.

How else could one describe the extraordinary process by which Mr. Kaplan had come to the conclusion that if a pronoun is a word used instead of a noun, a proverb is a pronoun used instead of a verb? It was outlandish, of course, and yet—when Mr. Parkhill had asked Mr. Kaplan, rather severely, if he could give one single example of a pronoun used instead of a verb, Mr. Kaplan, transported by that special joy that possessed him *in statu pupillari*, exclaimed, "Soppoze in a rizort hotal is sombody hollerink: 'Who vants to svim?' T'ree pipple enswer: 'I!' 'Me!' 'You!' All pronons. No voibs."

Surely a student could not be permitted to go on that way, changing the tongue of Chaucer and Swift and Hazlitt as he went along. But if a student refused to accept authority, the testimony of experts, the awesome weight of precedent, to what higher court could one possibly appeal? There was the rub.

Mr. Kaplan did not deny that English had rules—good rules, sensible rules. What he would not accept, apparently, was that the rules applied to *him*. Mr. Kaplan had a way of getting Mr. Parkhill to submit each rule to the test of reason, and Mr. Parkhill was beginning to face the awful suspicion that he was no match for Mr. Kaplan, who had a way of operating with rules of reason entirely his own. Only a man with rules of reason entirely his own would dare to give the opposite of "height" as "lowth," or the plural of "blouse" as "blice."

In trying to grope his way through the fogs of his ghastly dilemma, Mr. Parkhill had even taken Miss Higby into his confidence. "Miss Higby," he had said during a recess, while they were alone for a moment in the room that served as faculty refuge, "it might just be that one of my students is a—well, a kind of genius."

"*Ge*nius?" echoed Miss Higby.

"I mean, he seems to take the position that since he raises no objection to our rules, why should *we* object to—er—his?"

Miss Higby had made a sort of gurgling noise, saying, "We get an extra day of vacation this term," and hurried out of the room.

That remark had made Mr. Parkhill quite cross. It was not at all a matter of an extra day of vacation. Vacation had nothing to do with it. The trouble with Miss Higby was that, like Mr. Robinson, she simply refused to face facts.

They refused to face facts just as Mr. Kaplan refused to abide by the laws and the customs to which other people were beholden. He was a kind of anarchist. But that did not absolve the ANPSA of responsibility; it only added to its burdens. What Mr. Parkhill had finally decided was that if Mr. Kaplan refused to enter their universe, they would have to enter his. They would have to try to teach him, as it were, *from the inside*.

For there was no longer any doubt in Mr. Parkhill's mind that Mr. Kaplan did inhabit a universe all his own. That would explain how Mr. Kaplan had come to define "diameter" as a machine that counts dimes, and once dubbed the waterway which connects the Atlantic and Pacific "the Panama Kennel."

Mr. Parkhill passed his hand across his brow. He wondered if it might not be best to think of Mr. Kaplan not as a pupil but as some sort of cosmic force, beyond human influence, a reckless, independent star that roared through the heavens in its own unconstrained and unpredictable orbit. Mr. Kaplan was *sui generis*. Perhaps that was why he so often responded with delight, rather than despair, when Mr. Parkhill corrected him. It had taken Mr. Parkhill a long time to discover that Mr. Kaplan's smile signified not agreement but consolation.

One night Mr. Kaplan had delivered a rhapsodic speech on a topic which he had announced as "Amazink Stories Abot Names in U.S." New York, he had cheerfully confided to his comrades, was originally called "New Hamsterdam," Montana was so named because it was "full of montains," and Ohio, he averred, "sonds like a Indian yawnink." An Indian yawning…Sometimes Mr. Parkhill thought Mr. Kaplan would never find peace until he had invented a language all his own.

Ahead loomed the building in which the American Night Preparatory School occupied two floors. Tonight, bathed in gossamer moonbeams, it stood in ghostly grandeur. Mr. Parkhill removed his hat and went up the broad stone steps. Just as he was about to open the door, a voice behind him sang out, "Goot ivnink, Mr. Pockheel!"

He did not have to think or turn to know whose voice that was. No one else pronounced his name quite that way, or infused a routine salutation with the timbre of Archimedes crying "Eureka!"

"Vat's a madder? You not fillink Hau Kay?"

"I beg your pardon?"

"You vere lookink so fonny on de school."

Mr. Parkhill caught a glimpse of Mr. Kaplan's bland, bright mien, beclouded, for a moment, with solicitude. "It's nothing," said Mr. Parkhill hastily. "Nothing at all."

But he knew that he *had* been "lookink fonny on de school." He could have sworn that for a moment he had seen, glittering over the doorway:

> b. 25 years B.K.
> d. "?"years A.K.

They entered the temple together.

Mr. K∗A∗P∗L∗A∗N *and the Unforgivable "Feh!"*

"*Fata viam invenient*," Mr. Parkhill thought as he called the beginners' grade to order. "Fate will find a way." Vergil—that was who had said it. It was a consoling thought; and for some reason Mr. Parkhill found himself clinging to it as he called the roll. "Mr. Keeselman?"

"Here."

"Mrs. Rodriguez?"

"*Sí!*"

"Mr. Scymzak?"

"Yah."

"Mr. Kaplan?"

There was no answer.

"Mr. Kaplan?" repeated Mr. Parkhill, looking directly at Hyman Kaplan, who was in his usual seat, right in front of Mr. Parkhill, in the exact center of the front row.

Still no answer.

Mr. Parkhill frowned. "Mr. *Kap*lan," he called firmly, forcing Mr. Kaplan's gaze to meet his own. Forced? No; Mr. Kaplan's eyes had been waiting for Mr. Parkhill's all the time. Once he was sure that Mr. Parkhill was observing his every movement, Mr. Kaplan narrowed his

41

eyes in the manner of a stern judge about to pass sentence on a particularly reprehensible criminal, turned his head to his right deliberately, fixed the student at the far end of the front row with a withering glare, and, in a voice freighted with warning, intoned, "Hymie Keplen is in place."

Mr. Parkhill adjusted his spectacles uneasily. "Miss Goldberg…" Mr. Parkhill did not like the look of things; he did not like the look of things at all. And from the buzzings and hissings and glances that sped across the room he knew that the class, too, had read the dire meaning of Mr. Kaplan's pantomime. That narrowing of the eyes, that lethal stare, that doomsday tone— to any who knew Mr. Kaplan these signified but one thing: Hyman Kaplan had issued that formal *caveat* which precedes a declaration of war. There could be no doubt about it. Whenever Mr. Kaplan bestowed so malevolent a glare on a colleague, it was for only one reason: his honor had been slurred, and demanded satisfaction in battle.

But who was the student at the far end of the front row? He was one Fischel Pfeiffer. He had been admitted, originally, to Miss Higby's class, but after the very first recess Miss Higby had escorted Mr. Pfeiffer into Mr. Parkhill's room, where, with excessive casualness, she had informed Mr. Parkhill that although Fischel Pfeiffer was a most rare and conscientious pupil, a scholar of undeniable promise, he was "not *quite* ready" for the heady heights of Composition, Grammar, and Civics. In Miss Higby's considered opinion, Mr. Pfeiffer needed basic "drill, drill, drill" where certain fundamentals of the tongue were involved.

During the whole of Miss Higby's recitation, Mr.

Pfeiffer had remained standing, silent, baleful, his lips pressed tight, his face all gloom. None but the blind could have misread his mood: Mr. Pfeiffer was mortified by demotion. He was a thin, dapper man with rimless glasses, a polka-dot bow tie, and a cream-colored suit the sleeves of which were as sharp as knives.

"We're glad to have you with us," Mr. Parkhill remembered remarking in a reassuring manner. (At least it reassured Mr. Parkhill; it made no dent on Mr. Pfeiffer's conspicuous discontent.) "Class, this is Mr. Pfeiffer, Mr.—er—Fischel Pfeiffer. Won't you take a seat, please?"

Mr. Pfeiffer lifted his eyes just high enough to survey the reaches of the Siberia to which he had been exiled.

"There is a place in the front row," said Mr. Parkhill.

Without a word, in his own miasma of humiliation, Mr. Pfeiffer started toward the empty chair at the far end of the front row. It was at that moment that Mr. Parkhill had felt a premonitory twinge. For in order to get to the seat at the end of the front row, Mr. Pfeiffer had to pass directly in front of Mr. Kaplan. And Mr. Kaplan, by leaning forward generously, had managed to follow the entire colloquy between Miss Higby and Mr. Parkhill with the most avid fascination....

As Mr. Pfeiffer crossed in front of Mr. Kaplan, that self-appointed protector of the weak and the homeless had sung out, "Valcome, Fischel Pfeiffer! Valcome to beginnis' grate!"

Mr. Pfeiffer had paused, eyed his unsolicited cicerone, and uttered a monosyllabic sound the mere recollection of which still made Mr. Parkhill's forehead damp: "Feh!" That was all he had said: "Feh!"

43

Now "Feh!" was an expletive Mr. Parkhill had heard before—but in the *corridors* of the American Night Preparatory School for Adults, never inside a class-room. The expression had, in fact, rather interested him: it was a striking example of onomatopoeia. Just as "moo" or "quack" or "coo" conveyed their meaning with supreme accuracy, so "feh!," however inelegant, was a vivid vehicle for the utterance of disdain.

"Feh!" The class had caught its collective breath; then all eyes turned from Fischel Pfeiffer to Hyman Kaplan, a man of the most delicate sensibilities.

His jaw had dropped; his cheeks had reddened in disbelief. "Feh?" Mr. Kaplan echoed dazedly. "*Feh?* For de *cless*?!"

"Our exercise tonight is Open Questions," Mr. Parkhill had announced quickly. Long, hard experience in the beginners' grade had taught him how to apprehend the first faint alarums of discord, and how to canalize aggression by diverting attention. "The floor is open, class. Any questions at all, any problems you may have encountered in reading, writing, con-versation. Who will begin?"

Up rose the hand of Sam Pinsky.

"Mr. Pinsky," said Mr. Parkhill lightly.

"I ebsolutely agree with Mr. Keplen!" proclaimed Mr. Pinsky stoutly. "A student shouldn't make 'Feh!' for—"

"*That*," said Mr. Parkhill crossly, "is not a question. Mr. Matsoukas."

Gus Matsoukas emitted his immemorial growl, consulted a dog-eared envelope, and asked his question. "Which is for describing furniture: 'baboon' or '*bam*boon'?"

"Mr. Matsoukas," said Mr. Parkhill, knitting his brow, "a ba*boon* is an animal, an ape, whereas bam*boo*, not 'bam*boon*,' is a—er—wood." Mr. Parkhill explained the difference between the anthropoid and the ligneous in patient detail. (Mr. Matsoukas, who customarily referred to his dentifrice as "toot ponder," had much to learn.) "Miss Shimmelfarb?"

"'Mail' in 'mailbox,' where you putting letters. Is this a masculine?" asked Miss Shimmelfarb.

"N-no," said Mr. Parkhill, and described the difference between the postal and the human. "Mrs. Rodriguez."

"Why 'scissors' have 'c' and 's' but no two 'z's?" asked Mrs. Rodriguez. "I *hear* 'z's!" (That dreadful word "scissors," Mr. Parkhill reflected ruefully, must have plagued every teacher of every course in English ever offered in any land or time.)

"I'm afraid 'scissors' is just spelled that way," said Mr. Parkhill, with genuine regret.

The students entered into Open Questions with zest. They loved Open Questions. It offered them freedom, amplitude, respite from the constricting ruts of instruction.

"What is the League of Women Motors?" Hans Guttman, a man devoted to learning, asked.

"Who is Hannahlulu?" chirped Mrs. Tomasic.

"What kind candy is 'valley fudge'?" Mrs. Yanoff inquired.

Mr. Parkhill had worked his way deftly through all these linguistic snares and swamps. He, too, enjoyed Open Questions—its challenge, its unpredictability; yet that night, he remembered, he had been unable to shake off a sense of foreboding. For in the caverns below

45

consciousness, the flatulent memory of "Feh!" still echoed. It was difficult enough to preserve decorum in a class torn by fierce vendettas, a class that included such antithetical types as Hyman Kaplan and Reuben Plonsky, or Mr. Kaplan and Carmen Caravello, or Mr. Kaplan and Miss Mitnick. To add to this scholastic powder keg so incendiary a type as Fischel Pfeiffer, a man foolhardy enough to give the affront direct to Hyman Kaplan—Mr. Parkhill had felt a surge of outright displeasure with Miss Higby.

But all that was behind him now, Mr. Parkhill reminded himself. This was two nights later. The roll had been called, the decks cleared for action. There was work to be done. Mr. Parkhill put his attendance sheet to one side, cleared his throat, pretended he had not noticed the mordant pantomime Mr. Kaplan had addressed to Mr. Pfeiffer, and announced, "I have corrected the compositions you handed in last Thursday, class, and one thing that stands out in my mind is the number of—er— *dangling participles*." He paused for the briefest moment to let this sink in. "I shall read some compositions— without identifying the authors, of course. Let's see how many of us recognize the errors...."

He launched his apprentices on a brisk quest for dangling participles which did not end until the bell rang for recess. And in all that time, Mr. Parkhill noticed with mounting uneasiness, Mr. Kaplan said nothing, and Fischel Pfeiffer sat wordless, stony and withdrawn.

After the recess, Mr. Parkhill announced, "Now, class, suppose we have a little exercise on—vocabulary."

"Vary useful," declared Mr. Plonsky, whose renown

as a jobber had made him the leading anti–Platonist of the beginners' grade.

"I like," said Mr. Studniczka.

"Ooooh," breathed Olga Tarnova from her reservoir of unutterable griefs.

"Pencils and papers, please. Everyone."

The room rustled like aspens under a high wind. Thirty-odd scholars opened brief cases, handbags, portfolios, shopping bags.

"I shall write five words on the blackboard," Mr. Parkhill said, picking up a piece of chalk. "Use each word in a sentence, a—er—full sentence, that is. Five words, therefore five sentences." He smiled. There was no harm in leavening the bread of learning with the yeast of levity. "Write your sentences carefully, class. Remember, I shall grade not just your spelling, but entire sentences—diction, syntax, punctuation...."

"Oy," moaned Mrs. Moskowitz, fanning herself with her notebook. It was arduous enough for Mrs. Moskowitz to spell one word right; to spell five words correctly, and put them into five whole sentences in which all the *other* words had to be spelled right, *and* selected properly, *and* fitted into the terrifying architecture of syntax—that, for Mrs. Moskowitz, was piling new Ossas upon already overburdened Pelions.

Mr. Parkhill gave Mrs. Moskowitz a therapeutic smile and turned to the blackboard. In large block letters, he printed:

1. CHISEL
2. LAMP
3. GROAN
4. POTATOES

5. CLIMAX

"Oy!" came from the unnerved depths of Mrs. Moskowitz once more.

"Moskovitz," called Mr. Kaplan, "you doink a lasson or givink a concert?"

"You have five minutes," said Mr. Parkhill quickly, wiping the chalk dust off his fingers. He moved down the aisle, nodding encouragement to a student here, alleviating anxiety in a student there, stiffening the morale of the faint of heart.

How pregnant the moment before commitment always was. The eyes of his neophytes were racing across the five words on the board, appraising them like frontiersmen in a trackless forest, alert to the dangers that might skulk behind the most innocent façade, on guard against linguistic ambushes, reconnoitering "chisel" warily, taking the measure of "lamp" in stride, hurdling the limpid "groan" to reach the obvious "potatoes," resting at last on the word Mr. Parkhill, with his unerring sense of the appropriate, had chosen to close the maze—"climax."

"I'm sure you all know the meaning of these words," said Mr. Parkhill.

"I'm not," wailed Mrs. Moskowitz.

"Come, come now, Mrs. Moskowitz. Try."

Mrs. Moskowitz heaved into the unknown.

Miss Mitnick bent her head over her notebook, the bun of her hair like a doughnut on the nape of her slender neck, and began to write with sedate dispatch. Mr. Plonsky unbuttoned his vest, cleaned his bifocals, uncapped his ball-point pen, shook it from the habit of years of uphill struggle with sterile fountain pens, and inscribed his first sentence on a letterhead of Statue of

Liberty Remnants, Inc. And Mr. Kaplan, ever undaunted, cocked his head to one side, repeated each word aloud in a clear, approving whisper, adding an admiring "My!" or "Tchk!" of homage to Mr. Parkhill's incomparable gifts as a teacher, exclaimed "Fife fine voids!" and shot Fischel Pfeiffer a glower designed to remind him of the riches the beginners' grade had always spread before the worthy.

Mr. Pfeiffer saw it not. After one deprecatory glance at the blackboard, the thin-lipped malcontent had set to work with absolute decision and startling speed. Before most of the students had even cleared the troubling reefs of "chisel," Fischel Pfeiffer slapped his pencil down and announced, with contempt, "Done!"

The appearance of an archangel would have caused no greater astonishment.

"Done?"

"Finished?"

"So *fest*?"

Heads were shooting up all around the room in wonderment.

"What we have here, a *ginius*?" asked Miss Goldberg, and consoled herself with a piece of chocolate.

"A ragular spid dimon?" Mr. Kesselman queried.

"Pfeiffer expacts to graduate before midnight!" said Mr. Pinsky acidly, glancing toward his captain for approbation. Mr. Kaplan looked as if he had seen Beelzebub.

Before the sensation created by Mr. Pfeiffer's velocity had even spent its force, that fleet paragon stepped to the blackboard, seized a stick of chalk, and began to transcribe his sentences with careless disdain.

"We generally *wait* to go to the board until—" Mr.

Parkhill's voice trailed off.

Words were flowing from the end of Mr. Pfeiffer's chalk as if it were a magic wand.

In the congregation of watchers, all work ceased. The class sat transfixed. Then a chorus of "Oh !"s and "Ah!"s and "Fentestic!"s cleaved the air.

For on that plain, black board, in most beautiful script, a script both sumptuous and majestic, Fischel Pfeiffer had written:

1. In Chicago, pride Lake Michigan, many shops sell Mexocan jewelry made by small, sharp *chisels*.

A new hymn of admiration ascended from the seated—not only for the exquisite calligraphy, which would have done credit to a Persian, but for the mettle of a man intrepid enough to tackle as recondite a word as "Michigan," as exotic a name as "Mexocan."

"Dis man writes like an artiss!" cried Oscar Trabish.

"*Like* an arteest? No! He *is* an arteest!" flamed Miss Tarnova. Then she throbbed, "*This mon has soffert! This mon has soul!*" (Olga Tarnova, who considered herself a reincarnation of Anna Karenina, believed that all humanity could be divided into two categories: those with and those without "soul.")

A burst of glee issued from Mr. Blattberg. "Kaplen, you watching?"

"Pfeiffer makes you look like a greenhorn!" jeered Reuben Plonsky, searching for his nemesis through his bifocals.

White, crestfallen, Mr. Kaplan said nothing. He was staring at the board—abject, incredulous—where Mr. Pfeiffer was finishing his second grand sentence:

    2. In Arabean Nights, famous story, is Alladin's wonderful *lamp*.

Now the "Oh!"s and "Ah!"s fell like a shower, garnished by a lone, reverential "Supoib!"

"*Mamma mia*," gasped Carmen Caravello.

"Pfeiffer, congradulation!" chortled Mr. Plonsky.

"Mr. Kaplan, what you see?" grinned Stanislaus Wilkomirski.

"Pfeiffer, you raddy for college!" cried Shura Gursky, carried away.

Mr. Parkhill tapped the desk with his pointer. "Now, now, class. Order…" But he was, in truth, as fascinated as his flock. And why not? The years in the beginners' grade had taught him to expect, for a sentence using "chisel," say, "I have a chisel," or "Give me chisels," or even "I like chisels." For a word like "lamp," Mr. Parkhill had long since become conditioned to sentences such as "Take the lamp," or "Who stole this lamp?" Into such a pedestrian world had come a Hector, a man who dared write "Arabean Nights" when the harmless "old book" would have sufficed; who did not flinch before Aladdin, where the timorous would surely have written "boy"; who even had the audacity to use an appositive ("famous story") he could have sidestepped entirely. It was indeed "supoib."

And while the murmurs of tribute were still rolling down the ranks, Mr. Pfeiffer transferred his three remaining sentences to the board with a celerity that was to become a legend in the American Night Preparatory School for Adults:

3. Life is not only suffring and *groans*.
4. No one finds diamonds in *potatoes*.
5. What is Man? A bird? A beest? No! A *climax*.

To a symphony of praise as fulsome as any Mr. Parkhill had ever heard in a classroom, Mr. Pfeiffer turned from the board, stifled a yawn, and returned to his seat.

"Oh, Mr. Pfeiffer," sighed Miss Mitnick.

"Wohnderful," crooned Olga Tarnova. "*Khoroscho* for an arteest!"

"Keplan," mocked Mr. Plonsky, "you have nothing to say? Not a single criticize?"

Not only had Mr. Kaplan nothing to say, he seemed to be in a state of shock. And Mr. Parkhill felt vaguely sorry for him. True, a man with so reckless a confidence, so luxuriant an ego, might well be exposed to occasional reverses; still, Hyman Kaplan had a certain flair, a panache not often seen among the earthbound.

"Time is slipping away, class," said Mr. Parkhill. "We are not—er—finishing our assignments."

They sighed and stirred and resumed their labors, and soon Mr. Parkhill sent a contingent of six to the board. They copied their sentences soberly, dutifully, but the heart seemed to have gone out of them. They wrote without that spirited counterpoint of comment or soliloquy which usually enlivened performances at the blackboard. For over all their heads, like an unscalable summit, shone the glittering handiwork of Fischel Pfeiffer.

How feeble, by comparison, seemed Mr. Marschak's "Actors give big *groans*," how lackluster Miss Gidwitz's

"By me are old *lamps* the best," how jejune even Mr. Scymzak's brave foray into aesthetics: "Any piece Hungarian music has glorious *climax*." With apologetic gestures and self-deprecating shrugs, the listless six shuffled back to their places.

"Good!" said Mr. Parkhill brightly. "Discussion... Miss Ziev, will you read your sentences first?"

Miss Ziev, who had been quite vivacious since her engagement to a Mr. Andrassy in Mr. Krout's class, read her sentences *sans esprit*—and the discussion thereof died stillborn. Not a spark of life was struck by even Miss Ziev's "The boy has certainly *groan* lately."

Mr. Marschak followed Miss Ziev, and the discussion was as spiritless as the utterances of a stricken child. No outburst of "Mistake!" or "Hoo ha!" greeted Mr. Marschak's "He eats fright *potatoes*."

Mrs. Rodriguez followed Mr. Marschak, and once again Mr. Parkhill, unable to put heart into his charges, had to carry the entire discussion by himself—even unto Mrs. Rodriguez's defiant "Puerto Rico has nice, hot *climax*!!!"

"Miss Gidwitz, please."

There was but desultory response to Miss Gidwitz's "Mary had a little *lamp*."

An equally pallid reception greeted even Mr. Pinsky's unprecedented use of the word "chisel." (Mr. Pinsky, who seemed to consider "chisel" the diminutive of "cheese," had written: "Before sleep, I like to have a little milk and *chisel*.")

It was Mr. Parkhill alone who pointed out lapses in diction, the stumbling of syntax, the neglect of prepositions. The spirit of discussion had fled the beginners' grade. Gone were the *sine quibus non* of

debate: strong convictions, stanchly held; the clash of
opinions bravely defended; the friction of one certain
he is right rubbing against another positive he is wrong.

Now only Mr. Pfeiffer's sentences remained to be
read. Mr. Parkhill teetered back and forth on his heels.
"Mr. Pfeiffer."

A hush fell upon the classroom. All waited. All listened. And what all heard, in utter astonishment, was
the high, thin voice of Mr. Pfeiffer reciting in shrill
sibilance: "In Sicago, pride Lake Missigan, many sops
sell Mexican joolery made by small, sarp *tzisels*." There
was no getting around it: Mr. Pfeiffer had said "Sicago"
for "Chicago," "Missigan" for "Michigan," "sarp" for
"sharp."...

"A Litvak!" a clarion voice rang out. It was Mr.
Kaplan, rejuvenated. "Mein Gott, he's a Litvak!" He
wheeled toward Mr. Parkhill. "Must be! Fromm
Lit'uania! He pronounces 'sh' like stimm commink ot of
a pipe!"

The heavens opened above the beginners' grade.

"Shame, Koplan, shame!" howled Miss Tarnova.

"Can Pfeiffer *help* he is a foreigner?" protested Mr.
Trabish.

"In class is no place to condemn!" shouted Mr.
Plonsky, so agitated that his glasses almost slipped off
his nose.

"I *described*," said Mr. Kaplan icily, "I did not
condamn."

The riposte only fanned the flames that swept
through Fischel Pfeiffer's defenders.

"Not fair!" charged Mr. Blattberg hotly.

"Not fair?" Mr. Kaplan echoed. "If a customer calls
vun of your shoes a 'soo' vould you give him a banqvet

entitled, 'Hoorah! He's ruinink de lengvidge!'?"

"But discussion should be about the *work*," Miss Mitnick pleaded, "not the personal."

"Mine remocks are abot de prononciational, not de poisonal!" rejoined Mr. Kaplan.

"Class, *class*," Mr. Parkhill kept saying, "there is no reason for such—"

"Kaplan, *bad*!" blurted Mr. Wilkomirski. (Mr. Wilkomirski, who was a sexton, often confused error with sin.) "New man writes like king!"

"Ha!" cried Mr. Kaplan. "He writes like a kink but talks like a Litvak!"

"*Gen*tlemen—"

"Kaplan, you plaina jalous!" roared Miss Caravello.

"Who's makink poisonal remocks now?" asked Mr. Kaplan piously.

"Mr. Kap—"

"Stop! Caravello put her finger on!" boomed Reuben Plonsky. "Keplan picks on small ditail!"

"A mistake," said Mr. Kaplan, "is a mistake."

"Pfeiffer needs *praise*, not pins!" Miss Mitnick objected tearfully.

"Are ve in cless to praise—or to *loin*?" Mr. Kaplan flashed.

"You dun't give the Litvak a chence!" moaned Mrs. Moskowitz, all bosom.

"I vouldn't give an *Eskimo* a chence to drive 'sh' ot of English, eider!"

"Ladies—"

"You got to make allowance for frands!" stormed Mr. Blattberg.

"If mine own brodder makes a mistake," Mr. Kaplan retorted, "do I pretand he desoives the Nobles

Prize? If Pinsky makes a mistake, does Keplen say 'Skip, skip, he is maybe a cousin Einstein's'?"

"Gentlemen—"

"What's got Einstein to do with Fischel Pfeiffer?" asked Mr. Plonsky in bewilderment. "*Stop!*"

"Koplan, *you got no pity?*" importuned Miss Tarnova. "Piddy?" Mr. Kaplan drew erect, implacable in his wrath. "You esk piddy for *de man who sad 'Feh*!' *to de cless*?!"

Now Mr. Parkhill understood. Now the mainspring of Mr. Kaplan's wrath lay revealed. "Class!" said Mr. Parkhill severely. "There is no need whatsoever for such intense dispute. Nothing is to be gained by—er—passion. We are—" The upraised hand of Mr. Pinsky caught his eye. "Yes?"

"How do you spall 'passion'?"

Mr. Parkhill cleared his throat. " 'Passion,' " he said, regretting his impulsiveness. " 'P-a-s-s-' "

Before he could complete "passion," the bell rang. The contesting students rose, assembled their effects, and began streaming to the door, arguing among themselves, calling the familiar salutations. "Good night, all." "A *good* lasson!" "Heppy vik-end."

It had been a difficult evening, Mr. Parkhill reflected, a most difficult evening. The road to learning was long and hard, and strewn with barriers of the unforeseen. He noticed Miss Mitnick approaching the chair of the man who, responsible for all the tumult and the shouting, had been entirely forgotten in the heat of battle.

"Mr. Pfeiffer," Miss Mitnick blushed, "your writing is splendid. Also your sentence structure."

Mr. Blattberg joined them with a hearty "Pay no

attention to *Professor* Kaplen!" He twirled the gold chain from which two baby teeth dangled, and favored Mr. Pfeiffer with that half-fraternal, half-subversive smile he reserved for those he tried to recruit to the anti-Kaplan forces.

Then, to Mr. Parkhill's surprise, Mr. Kaplan stepped up to Mr. Pfeiffer, extending his hand in comity. "Pfeiffer, I congradulate. I hope you realize I vas only doink mine *duty*. I didn't minn to hoit fillinks."

"You sabotaged his self-respact!" hissed Mr. Blattberg.

"You made mish-mash from his recitation!" Mr. Plonsky glared.

"You—you acted *hard*," Miss Mitnick stammered, biting her lip.

Mr. Pfeiffer adjusted his bow tie nattily. "If you esk me," he said, "Mr. Kaplan was right."

"Hah?"

"*Who?*"

"Keplan?!" The Blattberg-Mitnick-Plonsky task force could not believe their ears.

"A mistake is a mistake," said Fischel Pfeiffer, quoting Mr. Kaplan *verbatim*, oblivious of the coals he was heaping on the heads of his partisans. "A fect is also a fect. I prononce bad."

"Pfeiffer, dobble congradulation on you!" Mr. Kaplan cried. "You honist! Batter an honist mistake den a snikky socksass! So you made a mistake! Who dozzn't? Still, you made on me a *fine* imprassion. Soch beauriful hendwritink! Not iven Mitnick writes so fency. So tell me, where you loined it?"

"I heppen to be in embroidery," said Mr. Pfeiffer.

"Aha!" Mr. Kaplan beamed. "Good night, Plonsky.

Good night, Mitnick." He went to the door, where he turned, narrowing his eyes as of yore, and said in a measured tone, "Ve can vipe ot de 'Feh!,' Pfeiffer. But vun ting you should know: You ken write like Judge Vashington, you can spall like Vinston Choichill, but ve got a *titcher*, Pfeiffer, a movellous titcher, who onlass you prononce 'sh' like a mama to a baby an' *not* like you booink at a ball game, vill kipp you in beginnis' grate if it takes fifty yiss!" He was gone.

As Mr. Parkhill locked his desk, he had the uneasy feeling that Mr. Kaplan was right, and hoped against hope that he was wrong. Fifty years...! Unless—yes— *Fata viam invenient*.

H∗Y∗M∗A∗N K∗A∗P∗L∗A∗N,
Samaritan

"Yas, it was romahnteek, but trahgic. The day and the night, the week ahfter the week, dear Father prayed for Nicolai—"

"Miss Tarnova," Mr. Parkhill interrupted gently. "In English, we say 'day and night,' not '*the* day and *the* night.' Watch those definite articles…"

Olga Tarnova's long lashes fluttered in gratitude. "Dear Father want to church to pray, to find the hope for end of ravolution—"

Mr. Parkhill cleared his throat. "It's 'hope,' not '*the* hope,' and '*the* end,' not 'end.' You seem to use the definite article when it is not required, and I'm afraid you omit it when it—er—is."

Olga Tarnova's dark eyes smoldered in despair. "In school, dear brohther, Alexahnder Ivanovich, always soffering, said us—"

"*Told* us, Miss Tarnova."

Miss Tarnova moaned; she was not made for the rarefied air of higher learning. "Pardone, pardone…" She smoothed her cobalt hair with a gesture that would have done credit to Camille. "Alexahnder Ivanovich *told* us not worry. So we try to altogather forgat."

"To forgat altogadder!" Hyman Kaplan sang out,

59

polite but decisive.

Miss Tarnova surveyed him coldly. "—To altogather forgat!"

"To forgat altogadder!"

Miss Tarnova stamped her foot. "How *I* said? *To altogather forgat!* What is matter?"

"Tsplit infinitif!" exclaimed Mr. Kaplan triumphantly.

Mr. Kaplan had, by supreme concentration, memorized three axioms anent English grammar, and he clung to them as cosmic verities: "Wrong tanse!," "Dobble nagetif!," and "Tsplit infinitif!" (Mr. Parkhill had had a difficult time persuading Mr. Kaplan to say "tsplit infinitif" instead of "tsplit infini*ty*." There was something about "tsplit infinity" which had rung bells of recognition in Mr. Kaplan's soul.) Whenever the opportunity arose to use one of these three precious *obiter dicta*, Mr. Kaplan, ecstatic, would seize it. "Tsplit infinitif!" he cried, and the walls resounded with its majesty.

Miss Tarnova's nostrils flared; her ophidian eyes burned; she flung out her arms, the gewgaws on her wrist jangling, and stamped her foot again. "Article—not article—dafinite, indafinite—splitting finitive! I am *Rossian*! I say what is in *heart*! *Nitchevo!* I stop!" She seared Mr. Kaplan with the glare of a Romanoff accosted by a *moujik* and flounced to her seat, a flame.

"Miss Tarnova..." Mr. Parkhill began soothingly. "If you —" But it was too late. Miss Tarnova was waving her hands in mute umbrage, inviting Mr. Plonsky and Miss Mitnick to avenge inequity most foul. Their minions promptly glowered at Mr. Kaplan, whose henchmen promptly glowered back and mobilized for combat.

Mr. Parkhill staved off the clash of arms. "I'm sure Mr. Kaplan meant no harm," he said earnestly. "He only tried to help...."

The passionate "Rossian" tossed her sultry head and breathed fire.

"Won't you go on?" asked Mr. Parkhill hopefully.

Olga Tarnova cast a dolorous glance at the heavens and, in a cavernous voice that dripped *Weltschmerz*, mur-mured: "Other time, be so good. Other time."

"*Som* odder time," Mr. Kaplan said politely.

A rich Slavic oath crossed Miss Tarnova's cherry lips.

"My!" Mr. Kaplan murmured in admiration.

Mr. Parkhill quickly called on Peter Studniczka.

It was the second Recitation and Speech period of the season. Mr. Parkhill had devoted most of the evening sessions to the sweet mysteries of Grammar, Vocabulary, and Sentence Structure. Recitation and Speech was an ordeal far greater than any of these, because of its intensely personal character, its pitiless exposure of the individual to public scrutiny, diagnosis, prescription, and autopsy.

It had opened rather well, with Mr. Hans Guttman, who had orated on the immortal Heine, whose songs ("in original Cherman") Mr. Guttman extolled as second to none. Miss Pomeranz had followed Mr. Guttman with a lively anecdote involving a *contretemps* whilst "shopping at Sex Fifth Avenoo." Mr. Scymzak had presented what first seemed an extravagant eulogy of The Netherlands —until a reference to the Savior made it clear that every time Mr. Scymzak said "Holland," which he pronounced "Holeland," he really meant "Holy Land," which he pronounced "Hollyland."

Then Miss Tarnova—how unfortunate that Olga

Tarnova had run head-on into both the definite article and Mr. Kaplan, and had capitulated under fire.

Miss Tarnova was the envy of every other woman in the class. Her voluptuous manner, her slumbrous eyes, her throbbing voice always sent sighs of longing through the female ranks. Perhaps it was not simply her airs, her eyes, her voice, Mr. Parkhill reflected; perhaps it was her perfume. Miss Tarnova, alone among the ladies in the beginners' grade, wore perfume to class—a particularly musky scent that whispered of a glamorous, if not downright lurid, past. Perhaps it was not the perfume either; perhaps it was Miss Tarnova's whole personality, which seemed overripe, beholden to a time when she had danced for princes of the blood, and men, driven wild by desire, had fought duels for her favor. Mr. Parkhill wished that Miss Tarnova would be a bit more restrained in her utterances, a shade less dramatic in her movements.

But this was no time for reverie. Peter Studniczka was trudging to the front of the room as if to the gallows: it was his début in Recitation and Speech. He stopped at Mr. Parkhill's desk, his head bent, his eyes glued to the floor. The perspiration on his brow was expanding at an alarming rate.

"Mr. Studniczka..." Mr. Parkhill said cheerfully.

Mr. Studniczka raised his head. He looked haggard. He was a quiet, almost morose student who never raised his hand, never volunteered, rarely spoke a word, and treated homework like poison ivy.

"Er—you may begin, Mr. Studniczka." Mr. Parkhill nodded encouragingly.

The last vestige of color deserted Mr. Studniczka's cheeks. He clutched his tie. (Mr. Studniczka often wore a blue work shirt, *without* a tie, to class.) His eyes went into a glassy glaze. He opened his mouth. "Lds gntlmns I lk Nv—"

The words, if that was what they were, died in a gurgling, vowelless stew. Then silence swallowed the gurgle. Someone coughed. Silence washed the echo away.

"A—er—little *louder*," said Mr. Parkhill bravely. "Do go on...."

Ghastly, drawn, the petrified pupil fixed his eyes, hosts to terror, somewhere between Arcturus and the top of Mrs. Yanoff's head. He parted his lips: they were so parched they sounded like paper rustling. His tongue clucked dryly. No words came out.

Mr. Parkhill kept smiling and nodding and broadcasting symbols of encouragement. Miss Mitnick fumbled for a handkerchief. Miss Goldberg strengthened her nerves with a nougat. Miss Caravello resorted to prayer.

Suddenly, from his seat in the middle of the front row, Mr. Kaplan whispered, "Mister, jost *talk*. Ve all your frands, your *pels*."

Out of the shroud that covered him, Peter Studniczka searched for the stranger.

"Tseasy! An' efter all—" the self-appointed Samaritan insinuated "—voise den Tarnova you *ken't* be!"

Miss Tarnova's impure rejoinder broke the verbal log jam: Without warning, in one continuous, breathless torrent, unbroken by the slightest pause or beat or cadence, Peter Studniczka, *in extremis*, blurted: "Ladies gantlemans I lak Nev York is fine place good eat also good work I buy suits with pants two for one I see nice in movie pic' for have new glass for eye to look at

America more good as Dubrovnik not sorry come try marry good lady cook wash to hev childs boy name Frank boy name Dinko also girl not care how name thank you please."

And like a tornado which had ripped into the room from the beyond, shattering the silence in one swirling gust, and roared away to leave a silence more ominous than before—Peter Ignatius Studniczka, unburdened of speech, stumbled back to his seat.

Mr. Parkhill did not stir. The eyes of his charges remained rooted to the spot where Mr. Studniczka had played Demosthenes: Mr. Pinsky looked dazed, Miss Ziev as if she had seen a ghost; Mrs. Tomasic breathed asthmatically; Miss Mitnick's compassionate handkerchief was arrested in mid-air; Miss Tarnova was so astonished that she neglected to flutter her lashes in astonishment. Only Mr. Kaplan seemed alive in the beating silence, celebrating the maturing of his ward.

"Er—" Mr. Parkhill said at last. His voice sounded as if it were under water. "Corrections, class?" No sooner had he said it than he realized its futility. The beginners' grade was immobilized.

"*No* corrections?"

Mr. Blattberg mastered his vocal cords. "The speech was so *fest*...."

Timid murmurs signaled assent. "Yeh," averred Miss Goldberg.

"Hard to understan'," muttered Gus Matsoukas.

"Ha!" cried Mr. Kaplan. "It vas movellous!"

"Too fast," Cookie Kipnis protested.

"Ve livink in an aitch of speed!" Mr. Kaplan retorted.

"No unnastan'!" Carmen Caravello complained.

"Go to a ear spacialist!" Mr. Kaplan stormed.

"Not good," mourned Olga Tarnova. "Too long. Was all same santence."

"*You* should make op soch a santence!"

Peter Studniczka stared at the calluses in his palms.

"Are there any *specific* corrections?" asked Mr. Parkhill hopefully.

Mr. Kaplan smiled his most debonair smile.

Up went the hand of Reuben Plonsky. Mr. Kaplan's smile melted.

"Even if was too fest," said Mr. Plonsky smugly, "*I* have soitin corractions." He placed his notes within an inch of his nose and peered through his bifocals. "Was missing 'the' and 'a,' also 'and.' Some verbs was in prasent for past and in past for prasent, and futures didn't exist at all. 'Nev York' isn't 'New York,' and 'Thank you please' in last place wasn't good in the foist place!"

Around this staggering feat of criticism the pro-Plonsky legions rallied. "Yah...Sure...Dozens mistakes!"

Mr. Kaplan's face was a cloud.

"Well, class," Mr. Parkhill ventured, "Mr. Plonsky has provided us with quite a list of—er—errors. Perhaps we should—"

Achilles' voice cut through the air. "It vas a movellous spitch! Strong! Prod! Foist-cless! *I* vant to say a few voids!" Up rose Hyman Kaplan.

"Mr. Kaplan, I'm afraid it is not your turn—"

"So lat dis be *mine* spitch!" Three strides had taken Mr. Kaplan to the front of the room. He shot his cuffs, buttoned his coat as if buckling on his armor, cast a scathing glance at the infidels, and declaimed, "Ladies an' gantlemen an' Mr. Pockheel! Vat's de minnink

Jostice?"

A hush fell upon the battalions.

"Jostice? J-O-S-T-I-S. Vat it minns?"

Miss Kipnis gaped at the champion of "jostice" and moistened her lips. Mr. Studniczka, who had not once lifted his eyes, fumbled with his tie. Miss Shimmelfarb nudged Mrs. Moskowitz, who was sound asleep.

"I'll tell you. Jostice is de finest, most beauriful emotion fromm human beans. It's nauble, sveet, good. It's liftink op humanity!" (Mr. Kaplan, indeed, seemed to be lifting up with the very words: he spoke from raised heels.) "Do *enimals* have Jostice? No! Are *sevages* havink? No! Den who got? Tsivilized pipple!"

"Mr. Kaplan—" Mr. Parkhill interposed.

But Mr. Kaplan, Jovian in wrath, had soared ahead. "Vy ve all came to vunderful U.S.? Becawss here is stritts pasted mit gold? Ha! Becawss ve vant to gat reech all of a sodden? No. So vy ve came to Amarica? For vun plain rizzon. Becawss here ve got Friddom! Here ve livink like brodders! 'Vun nation, inwisible, mit Liberty an' Jostice free for all'!"

Bright was the light in Molly Yanoff's eyes, deep the glow on Sam Pinsky's cheek.

"So alonk comms a fine man like Studniczka" (Mr. Studniczka looked up, aghast, at the sound of his name) "an' he gats op to make his foist spitch, to give a semple his English ve should all halp him ot. An' vat he gats? Sympaty? No, mine frands. Unnistandink? No, fallow-students. Jostice? No, beginnis' cless! He gats fromm *soitin* pipple—" Mr. Kaplan froze the blood of those unnamed souls "—shop voids, high-tone crititzizink, smot-elick ection! Batter *ashame* should dose soitin pipple be!" Several of them, indeed, were already writing in the hell to which Justice Kaplan had consigned them.

He paused for breath. His voice dropped. He turned to Mr. Plonsky, honey on his tongue. "Podden me, Plonsky. How lonk you in U.S.?"

Mr. Plonsky blinked myopically, but did not answer.

"Mine dear Plonsky, it's only a tsimple qvastion," Mr. Kaplan murmured. "Ufcawss, if you tong-tie…"

"Nine years," growled Mr. Plonsky.

Mr. Kaplan nodded. "Nine yiss…My! *Nine* yiss!" He seemed to be relaying the information to his Muse. "Not vun, not fife, but nine yiss!" His eyes flashed. "An' still only in beginnis' grate!"

Mr. Plonsky gasped, turned his back on Mr. Kaplan in insult supreme, and clutched his forehead.

"Studniczka, how lonk *you* in U.S.?"

All heads turned to Peter Studniczka. All ears pricked up. Mr. Studniczka was studying his thumb.

"Plizz, Studniczka," called Mr. Kaplan. "You got to *halp* Keplen. Like your lawyer." The thought pleased him. "So how lonk *you* in America?"

"Two year," mumbled Mr. Studniczka.

Mr. Kaplan uttered a cry of pure rapture. "Only two yiss? An' also in beginnis' cless! Studniczka, you Hau Kay! You vill—"

"Stop!" roared Mr. Plonsky, addressing the rear wall. "How long are *you* in America?"

"*I'm* comparink!" thundered Mr. Kaplan.

The bell rang. It rang with particular authority this night. Without another word Mr. Kaplan marched to his seat, a Galahad.

The scholastic synod milled around, arguing among themselves, lamenting Studniczka's prospects for the future, commiserating with apoplectic Plonsky, predicting a fate fair or foul for Hyman Kaplan, collecting their hats and coats to file, at last, through the door, trailing farewells to Mr. Parkhill.

"Good night…" he responded. "Good night…" He watched them diminish by pairs. He had hoped to have a word with Mr. Kaplan, alone—to urge upon him the self-discipline of restraint, to warn him against future philippics of so vehement a character, however fraternal his motives.

But Mr. Kaplan, transported by his triumph, was halfway out of the room; and on his very heels, like a grateful dog, was Peter Studniczka. Just before they passed out of Mr. Parkhill's hearing, he heard Mr. Studniczka say, "Mister."

Mr. Kaplan turned his head.

"Mister. You talk good."

Mr. Kaplan studied his acolyte for a moment. "*Me?*" he shook his head. "It's to leff. You know how lonk *I'm* in America?"

Mr. Studniczka did not reply.

"Fiftin yiss!"

"You talk good," said Mr. Studniczka.

Mr. Parkhill turned off the lights.

Mr. K*A*P*L*A*N *and the* Glorious Pest

" 'Then, amidst a breathless hush,' " read Mr. Parkhill, amidst a breathless hush, " 'Patrick Henry took the floor. All eyes turned to the fiery young lawyer, who thereupon delivered the most scathing attack on monarchy yet heard in the Virginia House of Burgesses: "Caesar had his Brutus, Charles the First his Cromwell, and George the Third"—cries of "Treason! Treason!" interrupted him— "and George the Third may profit from their example! If this be treason, make the most of it!" ' "

"Hooray!"

"Vunderful!"

"Dat's de way to talk!"

Mr. Parkhill lowered the text. He felt pleased, not only because the historic words always stirred his senses, but because the beginners' grade, having listened with such intensity of interest, had responded with such amplitude of feeling. "That, class, was one of the most dramatic moments in the history of the thirteen colonies. Ten years later, Patrick Henry delivered another speech, which is even more memorable. It has, indeed, become one of the truly—er—immortal orations in history." He closed the book. He needed no lifeless text to prompt him in that glorious peroration: " 'Is life so dear, or peace so sweet, as to be purchased at the price of chains and slavery? Forbid it, Almighty God!' " He paused. " 'I know not what course others may take, but as for me—give me liberty or give me death!' "

If his disciples had applauded Patrick Henry on Monarchy, they brought the rafters down for him on Liberty.

"Hoorah!"

"T'ree chiss for Petrick Hanry!"

"*Bravo! Bravo!*" Miss Caravello was practically on her feet, leading a parade. "Justa like Mazzini!"

"Ha!" Mr. Kaplan's scorn cracked out like lightning. "How you ken compare a Petrick Hanry to a—*vat* vas dat name?"

"Mazzini! Greata man! Botha patriot!"

"If in Italy dey had Petrick Hanry bifore, dey vouldn't have Mussolini later!" Mr. Kaplan flung his hand up in grandiose command. " 'Give me liberty—or give me dat!' "

"Good fa you!"

"Hoo ha!"

"Keplen, you should go in politics!" Mr. Pinsky cried, then slapped his cheek with a resounding "Pssh!" of admiration.

"Class…" Mr. Parkhill had to rap his pointer on the desk quite loudly before he could still his fledglings' ardor. (When the tribute due Patrick Henry was being accorded Hyman Kaplan, who had managed to utter the deathless words as if he were making them up on the spot, it was clearly time to intervene.) "I shall now assign your homework."

Out came pencils to record, and notebooks to receive, Mr. Parkhill's instructions. As the Spartans before Leonidas at Thermopylae, or the proud French legions before their Corporal at Marengo, so the beginners' grade of the American Night Preparatory School for Adults hearkened to Mr. Parkhill.

"During this semester," he began, "we have had occasion to discuss many different incidents in American history. We have not done this in—er—chronological order, because I have tried to answer your questions as they arose. Besides, as you all know, American History is taught in Mr. Krout's grade." He did not stress the fact that Mr. Krout lay beyond the forbidding stretches of Miss Higby. "So it is that we discussed Woodrow Wilson, say, before we even mentioned the Monroe Doctrine; or Thomas Paine before some of you even knew about Pocahontas." He smiled; it did sound amusing put that way. "In any event, we have covered quite a bit of ground. And so your assignment, for our next session, is—a composition on any famous figure, or any famous incident, associated with the American Revolution."

"My!" breathed Hyman Kaplan.

"Too hard," said Mr. Scymzak.

"I *lohve* American ravolutions!" announced Olga Tarnova, who hated the Bolsheviki.

Mr. Parkhill's most casual remarks sometimes had this electrifying effect—changing his students into Senators and the classroom into a forum. "A famous figure or incident associated with the American Revolution" elicited such a concatenation of approval and doubt, such cries of courage and groans of despair, that Mr. Parkhill felt as if he had not so much assigned an exercise as called a plebiscite.

71

"Foist-class assignmant!" beamed Mr. Kaplan.

"*Hard*," Mr. Scymzak repeated.

"Hod but good!" rejoined Mr. Kaplan. "Who vants izzy lassons? Izzy is for slowboats!"

" 'Slow*pokes*,' Mr. Kaplan."

A heartrending wail escaped from Mrs. Moskowitz. "Which figures? Which accidents?"

" '*In*cidents,' Mrs. Moskowitz, not '*ac*cidents,' " said Mr. Parkhill quickly. With Mrs. Moskowitz pedagogy was best practiced as if it were surgery: delay could be fatal.

"My mind is blenk about *in*cidents also," mourned Mrs. Moskowitz. "Please—give alraddy exemples."

A band of stalwart friends rushed to give her succor.

"Try crossing the Dalaware!"

"Take maybe Benjamin Frenklin?"

"Liberty Bells!"

Mrs. Moskowitz shook her jowls and groaned, wandering in Cimmerian darkness.

"Maybe John Hencock?"

"Spilling tea in Boston Hobber?"

"Don't shoot 'til their eyes toin white!"

Neither heroes nor events nor historic sayings could lift Mrs. Moskowitz out of the boundless mire.

"Mrs. Moskowitz," Mr. Parkhill began, "I—"

"Moskovitz, you not tryink!" cried Mr. Kaplan.

"Vat *am* I doing—skating?"

"You holdink beck de cless!"

"So go on witout me," howled Mrs. Moskowitz.

"You sebotagink our morals!"

" 'Mor*ale*,' Mr. Kaplan, not 'morals,' " said Mr. Parkhill anxiously. "Mrs. Moskowitz, I'm sure the assignment is not as difficult as you think." He gave her a smile intended to infuse confidence. "I'm sure that after you get home, when you have time to think about it, or review your notes, you will get *many*—er—ideas." He was not at all sure that Mrs. Moskowitz would get any, much less "many," ideas; if any idea was to become part of Mrs. Moskowitz' universe it would be because it found a way of taking possession of her, and not the other way around.

The hand of Barney Kesselman waggled in the air. "How long should be this composition?"

Mr. Parkhill weighed his next words carefully. "I do *not* want a long or—er—elaborate effort, class. Let's say, oh, not more than a page in length." He glanced at the clock on the wall, that third face between Washington's, from which he often drew resolution, and Lincoln's, to which he often repaired for condolence. It was two minutes to ten. "That is all for tonight."

Now, two nights later, in the solitude of his apartment, red marking pencil in hand, Mr. Parkhill was correcting their offerings. He did not know whether to feel pleased or disappointed. The prose of his novitiates was always full of surprises—some good, some bad; but this batch of papers contained so many surprises that it was difficult to think of them as either good *or* bad; they were just—surprising. History seemed to have plunged his pupils into the most extraordinary *personal* involvements.

Take Sam Pinsky, for example. Mr. Pinsky, a run-of-the-mill student, ordinarily did not let his reach exceed his grasp. This time, either inspired or intoxicated, Mr. Pinsky had thrown discretion to the winds. He had undertaken nothing less than a critique of the entire colonial policy of eighteenth-century England, and had become so incensed by what he called British "cold-heartiness" that he had soared into most untypical rhetoric:

> Colonists were starving, frizzing from cold, suffering like flys. But did British care? ? ? No! What they did? They made taxis.
> Taxis, taxis, taxis. On food. On tea. On sanding even a postal card to a dying mother.
> Oh, how foolish was Georgie III.

That was not at *all* the way Mr. Pinsky usually wrote.

Or take Mrs. Rodriguez. For some reason Mrs. Rodriguez had taken personal offense at General Cornwallis, whom, apart from labelling the blackest villain of the War for Independence, she blamed for not surrendering to Washington *soon* enough. Her composition was not so much an essay as an ultimatum, and Mr. Parkhill could not tell whether it had been designed to be descriptive of, or delivered to, the unfortunate Cornwallis.

Reuben Plonsky had penned a vitriolic essay on the Tories, whom he accused of crimes too heinous to be described, or, if described, to be spelled correctly. (It was hardly fair, for instance, to blame the Tories for "encouraging violins" when the worst that could be said about them was that they sometimes met persecution with viol*ence*.)

Mrs. Tomasic, whose Balkan forebears had survived oppressions beside which the Stamp Acts seemed philanthropic, had paid moving respect to that peerless seaman, "Admirable Grandpa Jones." Mr. Parkhill could see how a neophyte might confuse Admiral with "admirable," but how Mrs. Tomasic had alchemized "John Paul" into "Grandpa" he could not fathom.

After these erratic excursions into history, Miss Mitnick's measured words, always welcome, came as both a pleasure and a relief. Her composition was entitled "A Hero: Nathan Hale" and contained this moving passage:

> They tied his hands behind to hang Nathan. But brave, with his bare head he made that wonderful speech, simple and also poetical. "I regret I have only one life to give for the country." He was not maybe so important as Washington, but he is my hero. I admire.

Why, save for the occasional omission of a pronoun, that paragraph might have done credit to a veteran of Miss Higby's grade.

Mr. Matsoukas' paper, which he next assayed, had puzzled Mr. Parkhill. It had sung the praises of John Hancock whose aid to the cause of freedom, wrote Gus Matsoukas, no red-blooded American would ever "forge." It took quite a while for Mr. Parkhill to realize that Mr. Matsoukas had simply been careless; only a "t" separated "forge" from "forget."

Miss Ziev, from whom Mr. Parkhill had not expected to get any homework at all (Miss Ziev no longer wore the diamond ring given her by Mr. Andrassy), had come through with this:

MINUTE MEN
Farm men with long riffles. Always ready to fight. Did.

> Famous battel, with 1 shot whole world
> heard, was Battel of Grand Concourse.
> Good work, Ninute Men!

The only way Mr. Parkhill could explain how Concord
had become "Grand Concourse" was that some friend
of Miss Ziev who resided on that broad thoroughfare
had helped her with her homework.

Mr. Studniczka—Mr. Parkhill sighed. Peter Studniczka had submitted yet another of his cryptic sub-
stitutions for prose:

> 1776
> Best man — G. Washington.
> Bad man — King and Reps.
> Trators — Ben & Dick Arnold.
> Patroit — PULASKI FROM POLAND!

Mr. Parkhill was not happy about that paper. Something in Mr. Studniczka's mental processes seemed to
make him approach English vertically. Whether it was
because he actually *thought* in columns (which Mr.
Parkhill might understand were Mr. Studniczka, say,
Chinese), or whether he suffered from some sort of
phobia about whole sentences, horizontal sentences,
with a subject, verb, and predicate, Mr. Parkhill did not
know. He sighed again. Mr. Studniczka had a long way
to go—a long, *long* way to go. He corrected "trators"
and "patroit," and in the margin of Mr. Studniczka's
inventory wrote: "This is not a *composition*, Mr. S.
Please try whole sentences next time." He started to put
the paper aside, remembered something, and added:
"Ben*edict* Arnold. One man, not two." Then he picked
up the next composition.

Pellets of color flashed before his eyes. They came not from a pang of migraine, nor from retinal hallucinations; they came off the paper itself, from the title, which glittered with phosphorescent pride:

HAMILTON VERSUS JEFFERSON
A play!
By
H∗Y∗M∗A∗N K∗A∗P∗L∗A∗N

The irrepressible author had, of course, sought to immortalize his name by printing the letters in red, outlining them in blue, and distributing gay green stars between. Mr. Parkhill put the paper down and took a drink of water. He sharpened his marking pencil thoughtfully before picking up Mr. Kaplan's "A play!" again. This is what his startled eyes beheld:

> Hamilton: "The government should be
>   strong!"
> Jefferson: "No! Be ware strong govern-
>   ment. *People* must decide."
> Hamilton: "*People*? Ha, ha, ha, ha. Don't
>   trust people."
> Jefferson: "I TRUST! Also U.S. Mottoll,
>   saying 'God trusts.' O.K. *How's
>   about you*?"
> Hamilton: "You are a dreamy. Don't be so
>   nave."
> Jefferson: "Better to be dreamy. You are
>   against MAN!"

At this point Mr. Kaplan, tiring under the weight of Anglo-Saxon nomenclature, had dropped into abbreviations which may have lessened the strain on his fingers

but assigned disastrous connotations to his pro-
tagonists:

> Ham: "Every business needs a boss!"
> Jeff: "From bosses come Kings! Don't
>   forget!"
> Ham: "That's my last offer, Tom S. Jeffer-
>   son!"
> Jeff: "Same to you, L. X. Hamilton."

Mr. Parkhill felt a sharp pain in his head. He removed
his spectacles and rubbed his eyes. Something would
have to be done about Mr. Kaplan—about his spelling,
at least; a student simply could not be permitted to
wander around replacing hallowed names with
outlandish phonetic approximations. "Tom S. Jefferson"
indeed! "L. X. Hamilton..." The flashes now were not
occasioned by Mr. Kaplan's crayons.

"Good evening, class," said Mr. Parkhill pleasantly.
"I shall return your homework, first. Each paper has
been corrected and—er—evaluated. Please study the
red pencilings carefully. You can probably learn more
from your own mistakes than from almost any other
exercise."

Mr. Kaplan raised his hand; Mr. Parkhill braced
himself. "Y-yes?"

"You *liked* de homevoik, Mr. Pockheel?"

"Well," said Mr. Parkhill cautiously, "I think all of
you *tried* very hard. There were, of course, many errors
—too many, I fear. I shall now distribute—"

"Still, *som* homevoik maybe gave you a big soprise?"
suggested Mr. Kaplan confidentially.

Mr. Parkhill averted his gaze. He knew perfectly well

what Mr. Kaplan was driving at. Mr. Kaplan was trying to lure Mr. Parkhill into some compliment to the effect that imagination was more important than error, that one student had risen above his fellows by soaring into the empyrean of drama. Mr. Kaplan's pious expression even hinted that he would understand it if the public praises due such a genius omitted his actual name, which might incur the ire of the envious.

"Mr. Kaplan," said Mr. Parkhill firmly, looking his most faithful and difficult apostle straight in the eye, "the purpose of homework is not to 'surprise.' In fact, the best homework is the kind that, containing no errors, causes me no surprises whatsoever!" And with that *tu quoque*, Mr. Parkhill briskly proceeded to distribute the homework. "Miss Pomeranz…Mr. Trabish…"

Mr. Kaplan looked crushed. How, looking crushed, he also managed to convey the untarnished pride of one who has scaled Parnassus, albeit in vain, was something Mr. Parkhill would never understand.

"Miss Kipnis…Mr. Wilkomirski."

As the compositions streamed back to their creators, the sounds of illumination rewarded Mr. Parkhill for his labors.

"I spalled wrong 'Philadelphia'?"

"George is not Georgie…"

"Psssh! Was I wrong!" The resonance of a self-administered slap on the cheek told Mr. Parkhill that a dazzling light had dawned on Mr. Pinsky.

"Examine the corrections carefully, class. If you have a question, just raise your hand." Mr. Parkhill strolled down the aisle. There was a world of difference, pedagogically, between sitting at the desk and strolling down the aisle. The one was judiciary, the other egalitarian; the one enforced decorum, the other encouraged relaxation.

The next hour went so swiftly that the bell rang before anyone suspected it was time for recess.

And then, during the very closing minutes of the night, that crafty demon who confounds the plans of teachers no less than those of mice and men sent his seneschals among the innocent. Mr. Parkhill was conducting a spelling drill which he had himself devised, and of which he felt rather proud: twenty words containing "e-i-g-h-t" (from "freight" to "weight" via "height"), and twenty containing "o-u-g-h" (from "cough" through "rough" to "through").

He had just announced "Bought…thought…enough …" when Mrs. Moskowitz gave a cry of defeat, flung down her pen, and piteously appealed to Miss Kipnis beside her: " 'Enough'? *Enough!* Why dey dun't put in 'f' when is pronounced ffff? A mind crecks from soch torture, Cookie!"

"You got to be *patient*," sighed Cookie Kipnis.

"Don't give op!" called Rochelle Goldberg, fortifying her faith with a caramel.

"Learning takes *time*," pleaded Miss Mitnick.

They had reckoned without the defender of the faith. "Ha!" scoffed Hyman Kaplan. "U.S. vasn't fonded by sissies!"

"I dun't want to fond; I want to spall!" protested Sadie Moskowitz.

"Class—"

"Nottink good is izzy!" declaimed Hyman Kaplan.

"Eating is planty good, and planty easy!"

"You compare spalling to ittink?" Mr. Kaplan's expression set a new high for amazement. "You tritt

English like lemb chops?"

"The way *you* talk, it's chop suey!" stormed Mr. Plonsky, and his cohorts burst into laughter.

"Class, *class*," said Mr. Parkhill. "We are engaged in a spelling drill, not a debate!" He waited for the echoes of combat to die away, then addressed Mrs. Moskowitz sympathetically. "I can well understand how someone from another land must feel when confronted by some of the—er—peculiar ways in which our English words are spelled."

"*I* am fromm anodder lend," said Mr. Kaplan promptly, "an' still don't holler 'Halp!' "

"Mr. Kaplan," said Mr. Parkhill testily, "English *is* a most difficult language. And many of our words *are* spelled in most unreasonable—"

"Moskovitz can still make a good profit fromm odder pipple's semples," exclaimed Hyman Kaplan.

Mr. Parkhill looked up. What on earth was that? He frowned. "I beg your pardon."

Mr. Kaplan looked as blank as an oyster.

"I thought," said Mr. Parkhill, "I heard you say that Mrs. Moskowitz could—er—'make a good profit—' "

Mr. Kaplan nodded. "I mant like de Fonding Fodders."

This was too much for Miss Mitnick, who twisted her handkerchief and beseeched him, "What have Fonding Fathers to do with Mrs. Moskowitz?"

"It's obvious," said Mr. Kaplan carelessly.

"Ob—"

"*Mr.* Kaplan," Mr. Parkhill cut in dryly, "your comment is as unclear to me as it is to Miss Mitnick! I suggest you explain—no, no, you need *not* go to the front of—"

The admonition came too late. (Where Mr. Kaplan

was concerned any admonition seemed to come too late.) The bard of the beginners' grade was midway between his seat and his goal, that frontal zone to which some homing instinct irresistibly propelled him. He stopped, turned, and fixed Mrs. Moskowitz with narrowed eyes. "De Pilgrim Fodders didn't go back to England becawss dey had to spall 'enough'!" he cried, then transferred his scorn to Miss Mitnick. "Dey had beeger trobbles. Indians, messecres—"

"Mr. Kap—"

"—spyink fromm de Franch, poisicutions fromm de British—"

"Professor Keplan, stop giving a lecture in American history!" howled Mr. Plonsky, smiting his forehead.

"Stick to Mrs. Moskowitz!" shouted Mr. Blattberg.

Mr. Kaplan, a Triton among minnows, was deaf to their protestations. "An' ven de time came for de Amarican Ravolution, brave men like John Edems, Tom Spain, James Medicine—"

"It's Thomas *Paine*, Mr.—"

"—knew vas still missink a slogan, a *spok*! So along came Petrick Hanry." Mr. Kaplan's eyes went dreamy. "Dat vas a man....A prince! A tong like silver to kepture de messes!"

" '*Mass*es,' Mr. Kaplan, not—"

"An' Petrick Hanry vent into de Virginia House of Poichases—"

" '*Bur*gesses'—"

"—an' at vunce vas qviet, like de gomment district on Chrissmis Iv. So Petrick Hanry got don on de floor—"

" '*Took* the floor!' " Mr. Parkhill was getting desperate.

"*Took* de floor—denk you—an in beauriful voids, parful voids vhich comm don de santuries for all Americans who got true blood, he sad—"

"'True-*blooded*'—"

"'Julius Scissor had his Brutis, Cholly de Foist had his Cornvall, an' if Kink Judge got a bren in his had he vill make a profit from soch a semple!'"

Mr. Parkhill sank into his seat. *Expede Herculem.*

"Dat," Mr. Kaplan concluded, "also epplies to Moskovitz!"

"Omigott!" someone exclaimed.

"All I sad was 'enough' should have in it vun little 'f'!" wailed poor Mrs. Moskowitz.

"Koplen, you mad!" fumed Gus Matsoukas.

"This mon will change the heestory single-handed." That, perhaps the truest thought yet uttered, came from Olga Tarnova.

"I hoid enough," Mr. Plonsky groaned, and put his head between his hands.

"Mr. Kaplan…" Mr. Parkhill began. But he scarcely knew where to begin, so he began again. "Mr. Kaplan, I have rarely heard so *many* mispronunciations in so short a span of time." He knew he was being quite severe, but he did not shrink before stringent measures. "Charles the First is *not* 'Charley the—er—Foist.' Cromwell is *not* 'Cornwall.' And what Patrick Henry said was most certainly *not* what you quoted! There is a world of difference between 'George the Third *may profit from their example*' and 'George the Third can make a profit out of such a sample'!" Indeed, the enormity of the difference washed out of Mr. Parkhill's conscience the slightest vestiges of remorse for his tone. "Do you understand, Mr. Kaplan?"

Mr. Kaplan murmured "My!," expressing admiration, cocked his head, signifying attention, closed his eyes, indicating cerebration, opened one eye, denoting illumination, and said "Aha!", proclaiming conversion. Then, with a rueful but noble sigh, he started for his seat. "Still, I vill alvays edmire de glorious pest."

Miss Mitnick, who was getting more pale and more resolute by the moment, promptly protested: "Mistake! In pronunciation. '*P*ast' is not '*p*est'!"

Mr. Blattberg laughed, Mr. Wilkomirski guffawed, Miss Tarnova choked.

"Tonight is averybody an axpert?" Mr. Kaplan inquired caustically.

Tonight Miss Mitnick summoned all her courage to rejoin, "You don't have to be expert to know 'past' from 'pest'!"

A camel playing the bagpipe would have caused no greater sensation. The room rocked with merriment.

"Good for you, Miss Mitnick!"

"*Bravissimo!*" cried Carmen Caravello.

"You got Kaplen!"

"Et lest!"

Mr. Kaplan ignored the petty barbs and puny arrows, and turned to the one who had been foolhardy enough to give him the challenge direct. "Mitnick," he said pityingly, "you vould be corract, in usual soicomstences. But dis time, no. You are talking abot prononcink; *I* am talkink abot history."

" 'Past' *means* history!" Miss Mitnick said tearfully. "You said 'glorious p*e*st.' "

"Kaplen, give op!" crowed Mr. Blattberg.

"Keplan, sit down!" brayed Mr. Plonsky.

"Koplan wrong, wrong!" exultant Tarnova crooned.

"Mr. Kaplan," intervened Mr. Parkhill crisply, "Miss Mitnick is absolutely right. 'Past' refers to what has gone by. 'Pest,' on the other hand, refers to a—" An inner bell tolled a note of warning in his brain; an awful apparition congealed before his mind's eye; too late, too late. He did not need to hear Mr. Kaplan's next words to recognize the trap into which he, like poor Miss Mitnick, had so gullibly fallen.

"To a tyrant like Kink Judge," declaimed Hyman Kaplan, "vat else vas Petrick Hanry bot a glorious pest?"

After that, twenty words with "o-u-g-h" seemed an inglorious nuisance.

The Case for Mr. Parkhill

It was a miserable evening. All day long the rain had come down, in sudden, driving shafts, the way it used to descend upon Camp Quinnipaquig, the summer he had spent there as a counselor. Mr. Parkhill put on his rubbers and his Burberry, opened his big black umbrella, and sloshed through the streets. It was only two blocks to the little restaurant on Ninth Street, and when he got there he ordered half a grapefruit, the clam chowder, and the steamed Maine lobster. He desserted on a delectable deep-dish apple pie, and, because it was a special occasion, drank *two* cups of Sanka. It was his birthday.

He had received a lacy birthday card from his Aunt Agatha, mailed, as it was each year, so as to arrive exactly on date, and containing, as it did each year, a crisp five-dollar bill with the tart instruction: "To be spent on something *foolish.*" Aunt Agatha always underlined the "foolish."

The only other letter he had received (and what a surprise that had been) was from Mr. Linton, head-master of Tilsbury:

Dear Parkhill:
The other night Mrs. Linton and I were reminiscing

about past boys, and as we browsed through the old school annuals we came upon your photograph (the year you were awarded the Ernestine Hopp Medal for School Spirit). When Mrs. Linton reminded me of the time you astonished us all, as a freshman, by parsing that sentence from Cicero during tea, we laughed merrily.

The only other boy Mrs. Linton remembered so well was Wesley Collender ('33), who placed a copper contrivance in the fuse box at Farwell which intermittently expanded and contracted so that the "lights out" bell rang on and off, on and off, for a goodly ten minutes before Mr. Thistlewaite could ascertain the cause, and effect the remedy. Thistlewaite is no longer with us. He is, I believe, at Claremont or Carmel or some such place in the western states that begins with "C."

Be that as it may, Mrs. Linton called my attention to the birth date under your picture. "Why, that is next Tuesday!" she exclaimed, and indeed it was.

I extend, accordingly, our felicitations, and express our joint wishes for, in *loquendi usus*, "many happy returns."

Faithfully yours,
Amos Royce Linton

It had been awfully nice of Mr. Linton to write. Mr. Parkhill could not help feeling touched. The last time he had seen "Old Molasses," which was what the boys privately called Mr. Linton, was six years ago, when his class had presented the school with a fine, carved newel post for Modley Hall.

Mr. Parkhill remembered the first time he had gone back to visit Tilsbury. It was the year after he had received his B.A. When Mr. Linton had asked him what he was doing now, Mr. Parkhill told him he had taken a substitute teaching post, just for the experience, at the American Night Preparatory School for Adults.

"Parkhill," Mr. Linton had boomed in his no-nonsense manner, "what on earth is that?"

"It is a night school, sir."

"College entrances? Cram courses? That sort of—"

"Oh, no, sir. This is an elementary school."

"A *what*? Speak up, Parkhill!"

"An *elementary* school, sir," Mr. Parkhill repeated, raising his voice. "For adults."

Mr. Linton must have gotten hard of hearing, for he had gazed at Mr. Parkhill steadily for a moment and mumbled something that sounded like "Good God!" But that could not have been it; that was not at all like Mr. Linton; it was probably "Great Scott."

Mr. Parkhill often found himself thinking back to that little episode. He could understand that a man like Mr. Linton had no way of knowing what a fine institution the American Night Preparatory School for Adults really was. After all, Mr. Linton had led a rather sheltered life: Exeter, Harvard...He wondered, for instance, what Mr. Linton would have said when Hyman Kaplan named our leading institutions of higher learning as "Yale, Princeton, Hartford."

Tilsbury...What a different world that had been. What a different world it *was*. Mr. Parkhill felt a rush of pleasant, almost poignant, memories: that lovely campus, so tidy, green, serene, composed; the broad river that overflowed its banks in the spring; the school pond on clear winter days, a burnished white mirror; the path across Main Quad, that none but lordly seniors were permitted to use...Those were happy days in a happy world, a world ten thousand miles and years away.

Occasionally, Mr. Parkhill caught himself wondering what it would have been like if he had returned to Tilsbury as a master. (Mr. Linton had never even sounded him out on that, to be frank about it.) Life was so curious. Who would have thought that the teacher whom Mr. Parkhill had temporarily replaced at the American Night Preparatory School for Adults would never return? No one even knew what had happened to him.

Mr. Parkhill recalled how Aunt Agatha used to ask him, whenever he visited her, if he intended to spend the rest of his life "among those people in New York." Aunt Agatha, who had never even set foot in New York, did not understand the special rewards adults provide someone who regards teaching not as a job, but as a mission. He had once had a little fun at Aunt Agatha's expense by saying, "Why, Aunt Agatha, just as your father brought God to the heathen, I bring Grammar to the alien."

Aunt Agatha never brought the subject up again after that.

"Miss," Mr. Parkhill called.

The waitress, who had done everything well except wait, slouched toward him from the kitchen.

"Check, please." (For some reason, Mr. Parkhill remembered the night Mr. Kaplan, chivvied by his critics and cornered by his foes, who demanded that he explain the "R.S.V.P." he had, in a reckless burst of elegance, tacked onto a composition, rejoined, "It minns 'Reply, vill you plizz?'")

He paid his bill, put on his coat and his rubbers, stepped into the street, and opened his umbrella. The rain was, if anything, worse.

He began to walk quite briskly. He could hardly wait to get to the school. Sometimes, when he entered that old, unprepossessing building, he felt as if, like Alice, he was walking through a looking glass, into an antic and unpredictable world beyond.

"Miss Goldberg…Mr. Scymzak…Mrs. Rodriguez…"

As Mr. Parkhill called the roll he could not help noticing that Mr. Kaplan had not yet arrived. The seat in the exact center of the front row, that seat directly in front of Mr. Parkhill's desk, was empty. When Mr. Kaplan occupied that place, he seemed to loom out like a mountain, blotting out the rest of the class; and when Mr. Kaplan was not in that seat, as now, it seemed a good deal emptier than any other seat could possibly be.

"Miss Pomeranz…Mr. Wilkomirski…"

It was not simply that the corporeal Mr. Kaplan was missing; a certain point of view was missing, a magnetic pole, a spirit that expressed itself every moment the class was in session—with a gesture or a sigh, a whisper or grunt, a cluck, a snort, a gloat, a sneer, an approving "My!" or an admonishing "Tsk!," a commanding "Aha!" or a triumphant "Hau Kay!" Mr. Kaplan's "Hau Kay!" often sounded like a judgment from on high.

"Miss Mitnick…Miss Gidwitz…Mr. Kap—"

The voice of Sam Pinsky cut the fateful name in half. "Mr. Keplen asked me I should say he is onawoidably ditained. For maybe hefenarr."

Mr. Parkhill's long years in the beginners' grade had equipped him to translate "hefenarr," without the slightest break in his stride, into "half an hour." "Thank you." He put the attendance sheet to one side. "Well, class, suppose we devote the first part of the evening to—Recitation and Speech."

Smiles, grins and dulcet affirmations issued from the

Messrs. Plonsky and Marcus, and the Mesdames Gursky and Tomasic: They loved Recitation and Speech. Groans, moans and piteous suspirations drifted out of Mrs. Moskowitz and Peter Studniczka: They hated Recitation and Speech.

"May I remind all of you, once more, to speak slowly, carefully, enunciating as clearly as you can. Recitation and Speech can be one of our most valuable—"

"It gives me goose-dimples," wailed Mrs. Moskowitz.

"From prectice you will *learn*," attested Miss Ziev, gazing at the diamond ring with which Mr. Andrassy had re-pledged his troth.

"I should live so long." Sadie Moskowitz fanned her many chins with a notebook.

"Now, now, Mrs. Moskowitz," said Mr. Parkhill with a smile, "nothing ventured, nothing gained." And probably because of that note from Mr. Linton, *Empta dolore docet experientia* leaped into his mind. How appropriate: "Experience wrought with pain teaches." He noticed the hand of Oscar Trabish in the air. "Yes?"

"What it means?"

"I beg your pardon?"

"What it *means*?" Mr. Trabish repeated. (Mr. Trabish was a cleaner-and-dyer.)

Mr. Parkhill cleared his throat. "What does—er—what mean?"

"Those words you just gave. About adwentures and games—"

"Ah!" Mr. Parkhill could not help exclaiming. "I said, 'Nothing ventured,' not '*ad*ventured,' Mr. Trabish, 'nothing *gained*,' not—er—'games.' It is a saying. It means that if we never try, how can we hope to succeed?"

"Psssh!" cried Mr. Pinsky, closing his eyes and slapping his cheek with his palm. "Will Mr. Keplen be mat he wasn't here to hear those woids!"

"'*Mad*,' Mr. Pinsky, not 'mat,' " said Mr. Parkhill earnestly. "And it really would be better to say that Mr. Kaplan will be 'disappointed,' or 'sorry,' instead of 'mad.' 'Mad' means insane, or—er—crazy."

"Exactly the woid for Keplan!" grunted Mr. Plonsky.

"Wait till he *comms* before you insult!" said Mr. Pinsky indignantly.

Miss Caravello gave a derisive laugh. "Ifa Kaplan is scratch, Pinsky holler 'Ouch!' Ifa Kaplan is tickle, Pinsky makes 'Ha, ha!' "

Mr. Pinsky turned to Carmen Caravello and tried to bestow upon her that glare, compounded of ice and fire, with which he had often seen Mr. Kaplan freeze the blood of his foes.

"You look like Cholly Chaplin, not Hymie Kaplen," Mr. Blattberg snorted.

"Mrs. Yanoff," Mr. Parkhill called quickly, "will you go to the front of the room, please?"

A cantata of encouragement launched Molly Yanoff on her fearful path. She moved her chair, removed her glasses, smoothed her hair, soothed her morale, and proved her mettle by answering a question no one had asked: "So what's to be afraid?"

"Sure!" "Soitenly!" "Just stend op and talk!" the sympathetic gallery sang out.

"So what's the woist can heppen?" asked Cookie Kipnis.

"The woist can happen is I'll make four-fife mistakes," sighed the lady who always wore black.

This union of courage and stoicism brought a

medley of praises from the pit.

"Good fa you, Yanoff!"

"That's a spirit!"

Even Miss Mitnick, the shyest of gazelles, murmured, "Bast wishes."

Mrs. Yanoff marched to the front of the room with stately tread, placed one hand on the desk for support (it looked for a moment as if she were reeling, but she was only twisting or stretching), placed the other hand resolutely on a hip, and, in a surprising baritone, a voice before which both man and beast might quail, thundered, "Mary had a little lamb, with fleas white like snow!"

Mr. Parkhill sank into a chair at the back of the room. He saw Miss Gursky poise pencil over notebook, on the alert for error; he saw Mr. Scymzak put his hand over his eyes, the keener to attend; he saw Mrs. Moskowitz, reprieved from recitation, slide down her noiseless ways to somnolence. Recitation and Speech had, unquestionably, begun.

"This little kindergarten pome," Mrs. Yanoff announced, "is learned by—by all the little kitties in America. Just like my little goil, Hinda, age tan, also learned it. So why I am taking waluable time in Racitation and Speech to mantion this simple nurse's rhyme?"

"Why?" Tiny Tomasic promptly chirped.

"Because the woild would be a batter place all arond *if grownops behaved more like kitties*! Honist, sveet, and nice! If Congriss would be more like kindergarten, would maybe be less greft, crime and wiolence! Humans: remamber children!" And with that exhortation, her face flushed with both exertion and exaltation, Molly Yanoff marched back to her seat.

She barely had time to regain it before hands were bobbing up and down like buoys in a squall.

"Thank you, Mrs. Yanoff," said Mr. Parkhill. "Now —er—discussion."

Mr. Trabish opened the post mortem by observing that Mrs. Yanoff had used "goil" instead of "girl" and "woild" instead of "world." (Mr. Trabish had come a long way since his initiation into the beginners' grade.)

Miss Shimmelfarb remarked that Mrs. Yanoff had "used 'tan,' which is for color, instead of 'ten,' which is for aitch!"

Stanislaus Wilkomirski deplored the fact that Mrs. Yanoff kept saying "kitties" when she obviously meant "more than one children."

Miss Caravello leaped into the fray with a challenge to Mrs. Yanoff's naïve panacea for strife: anyone familiar with either children or kindergartens, Miss Caravello hotly observed, anyone not bemused by false sentiment, knew that our little ones would "chopa off da heads" of all within reach if but possessed of the weapons and provided with the opportunity.

"Cynic! Skaptic! Cynic!" hissed Olga Tarnova, thrice, then lamented, "You got no faith in *mon*? In God? In human *soul*?"

Miss Caravello cried "Name of the name" in Italian, and Miss Tarnova shot back an impure rejoinder in Russian, before Mr. Parkhill could impose an uneasy peace. (Tolstoy versus Machiavelli, he thought with a certain fascination.) "Let us limit our discussion to Mrs. Yanoff's *English*," he said earnestly. "There was one interesting mistake—in pronunciation—which has not yet been mentioned. It is most important. It occurred in Mrs. Yanoff's very first sentence."

His students dived deep into memory to recover Mrs. Yanoff's very first sentence. The diving was in vain.

"The sentence began," hinted Mr. Parkhill, " 'Mary had a little lamb…' "

The class wandered through the caverns of "Mary had a little lamb"—to no avail.

"Did anyone notice how Mrs. Yanoff *completed* that quotation?" Mr. Parkhill asked hopefully.

No one seemed to have noticed how Mrs. Yanoff had completed that quotation.

"Well…" Mr. Parkhill moistened his lips. "Mrs. Yanoff said that Mary's little lamb had '*fleas*' as white as snow!" He stressed the "fleas" quite emphatically.

"Maybe it was a *bleck* lamb?" ventured Fanny Gidwitz.

"In New York snow is not white!" Mr. Matsoukas, yearning for Arcady, declared.

"That is not what I mean." Mr. Parkhill sighed, and stepped to the board and printed:

FLEECE
FLEAS

Not a single scholar broke into the welcome responses to revelation. Not a single "Ah!" or "Oh!" or "Hoo ha!" ascended from the lyceum.

"Mary's little lamb," Mr. Parkhill frowned, "had a '*fleece*,' class, not 'fleas.' " He went on to delineate the disasters which might follow the replacement of the sibilant with the fricative. "Why, the entire meaning of a word, or a sentence, or an idea, can be radically altered if one says 'zzz' when one means 'sss,' or '*sss*' when one means 'zzz.' "

"You hear?" whispered Cookie Kipnis.

"Imachin," breathed Mr. Guttman.

Mrs. Moskowitz was snoring softly.

"For example…" On the board Mr. Parkhill printed:

PEAS
PEACE

"Ah!"s and "Ooh!"s and a reverent "Holy smoky!" from sexton Wilkomirski greeted "peas" and "peace."

Mr. Parkhill struck again, while the pedagogical iron was still hot. "Or these words…"

KNEES
NIECE

Now the class was beside itself with cognition.

"A niece and a pair knizz is som difference!"

"Just on accont one little latter!"

"Sss! *Zzz!*" went one group of students. "Zzz! *Sss!*" went another.

The room buzzed as from a swarm of energetic bees.

"And sometimes, class," Mr. Parkhill plowed on, exhilarated by success, "two words are spelled alike, exactly alike, yet are pronounced differently *and have entirely different meanings!*"

This, alas, was too much for the beginners' grade.

"Hanh?" cried Mr. Marschak incredulously.

"No," groaned Rochelle Goldberg, and consoled herself with a bonbon.

"Same word, same spell, no same mean?" was the

97

way Peter Studniczka put it.

Mr. Parkhill's chalk fairly flew across the slate as he printed:

CLOSE
CLOSE

He turned to the class: "Now these, for instance, are two entirely different words!"

At this point Mrs. Moskowitz, returning to sentience, saw "CLOSE" spelled twice on the board, heard Mr. Parkhill's "two entirely different words" and released a heartrending "Oy!"

" 'Clo*se*,' " said Mr. Parkhill anxiously, "is an adjective, which means near. But 'clo*ze*,' pronounced with the '*z*,' is a verb, which means to shut, as in 'Close the door—' "

As if in some perfectly timed dramatization in reverse, the door was flung open. All heads turned. There, his clothes dripping, his face wet but his smile incandescent, his glistening hair wreathed in a sort of halo from the light in the corridor beyond, stood—

"Mr. Keplen!" cried Sam Pinsky.

"Et lest!" grinned Fanny Gidwitz.

Not all his comrades greeted Mr. Kaplan in such joyous accents.

"About time!" scowled Mr. Plonsky, squinting at his watch to see what time it actually was.

"You had to stop maybe on the way at City Hall?" asked Mr. Blattberg scathingly.

"You arriving or leaving?" inquired Miss Gursky.

Mr. Trabish announced, "Mr. Kaplan isn't late; the class is *early*!"

Mr. Kaplan suffered these taunts nobly. "I couldn't find fest vat I vanted," he said mysteriously. "An' texis are scerce like a chicken's toot."

"Good evening, Mr. Kaplan," said Mr. Parkhill dryly.

It was just like Mr. Kaplan to enter a room that way. Any other student arriving this late would have courted invisibility, opening the door like a mouse, entering on tiptoes like a thief, creeping to the nearest vacant seat, speaking only if spoken to—and then only to mumble some agonized incomprehensibility. Not Hyman Kaplan. He could not even arrive late without endowing it with the attributes of a world première. He made his tardiness an occasion that called for public rejoicing.

Mr. Parkhill noticed that Mr. Pinsky was signalling to Mr. Kaplan with surreptitious flippings of his hand, accompanied by clandestine emissions of "Psst! Psst!" But Mr. Kaplan merely nodded with a certain insouciance and made not the slightest move to enter the room.

"Do come in," said Mr. Parkhill, not without a tinge of sarcasm.

"Axcuse me," said Mr. Kaplan; but his expression was not at all like "excuse me." "You blockink de dask."

Mr. Parkhill could hardly have been more astonished. He had indeed moved, without thinking of it, from the blackboard to the side of the desk nearest the door; but why that should impede Mr. Kaplan's passage from the door to his seat, a path entirely unobstructed by Mr. Parkhill *or* the desk, Mr. Parkhill could not for the life of him comprehend. "Mr. Kaplan," he began frostily, "I believe—"

He never finished the sentence. For the moment he turned, Mr. Kaplan lunged toward the desk, whipped a large object from behind his back, placed it on the desk with a flourish, and cried, "Soprise!"

The class, which had remained unusually quiet (now that Mr. Parkhill thought of it), erupted into salutations and applause.

"Congrejulation!"

"Happy boitday!"

"A hondritt more!"

Even Mrs. Moskowitz, returned from hibernation, sang out: "De present is from all!"

Mr. Parkhill felt his neck getting warm; a flush crawled up his cheeks. So that was why Mr. Kaplan was so late...and why he had made so odd an entrance...and why he had seemed so unapologetic. He had been shopping....But how in the world had they found out?

Mr. Kaplan was pointing to the parcel on the desk. "So open op."

"Let all have look," called Mrs. Rodriguez.

"Could be teacher already *has* it," Dostoevsky's daughter intoned in her customary premonition of doom.

"Impossible!" Mr. Kaplan glowered.

Mr. Parkhill realized that they were awaiting his every word. "I—er—well, class—" He cleared his throat. "I hardly know what to say."

"*You* don't know what to say?" echoed Miss Ziev in delight.

"Don't say. Enjoy!" called Stanislaus Wilkomirski.

Mr. Kaplan raised his hand imperially. "Procidd, Mr. Pockheel."

Mr. Parkhill fumbled with the wrapping on the parcel. It was gold-colored, with a bow of white ribbon the size of a cantaloupe, and wet, which made it singularly difficult to remove.

"Reep it!"

"Pull, maybe."

"*Cot!*"

"From de site!"

He removed the cantaloupe and the ribbon, and before the gold–colored paper came off the parcel, Mr. Parkhill suspected what was contained within. An attaché case. He pulled the last, damp strip of paper away. It was. An attaché case.

"Psssh!" cried Mr. Pinsky, slapping his cheek in ecstasy. "Is dat *beautful*!"

"Use in best of halth," called Miss Goldberg.

"*Bella! Bella!*" That, of course, was Miss Caravello.

Mr. Kaplan passed his lighthouse beam across the ranks before him and inquired, *sotto voce*, "How's abot mine choice?"

"Fine!"

"I gotta admit!"

"Poifict!"

Mr. Kaplan accepted their accolade and signalled for silence again.

All eyes converged on Mr. Parkhill. He wiped his palms. "Well, class, this is really very kind—"

"Mr. *Pock*heel," Mr. Kaplan cut in with the pained air of a Brahmin forestalling some ghastly breach of protocol, "de acknowledgink comms *efter* de prezan-tink!"

"Oh," said Mr. Parkhill. "Excuse me."

Mr. Kaplan faced his confreres, raised his arms to shoot his cuffs rather more ceremoniously than usual, inclined his head in the gracious manner of the Queen Mother distributing prizes at some rustic bazaar, and orated: "Distingvished titcher of beginnis' grate of Amarican Night Prap School for Adolts, prod mambers of de cless…" (Mr. Parkhill wondered why it had never occurred to him to call the ANPSA a prep school.) "Tonight ve have a fine, a foist-cless occasion. Soch occasion is comming only vunce a year to eny man, an' netchelly also only vunce a year iven to our lovely titcher!" Mr. Kaplan paused for the applause he deemed appropriate at this juncture; it came; it departed at a wiggle of Mr. Kaplan's forefinger. "Ve all like boitdays—espacially odder pipple's!" Mr. Kaplan bestowed a glance of rebuke upon Mrs. Rodriguez, with whom he had once locked horns over that vanity which impels women to tamper with chronology. "So tonight ve vill tsalebrate Mr. Pockheel's, in a briff ceremonia. Ve got no *program*, ufcawss. Still an' all—"

"Make short, in Gott's name!" Mr. Plonsky broke in, then turned to face the rear wall in a gesture of supreme disgust.

"The Declaration Constitution didn't take so long," exclaimed some secret member of the Plonsky-Blattberg cabal.

"Call Miss Mitnick," Gus Matsoukas muttered.

"Miss Mitnick!" "Rose Mitnick!" "Speech from Miss Mitnick!" came a dozen rebel cries.

Olga Tarnova waved her perfumed handkerchief.

"You'll *gat* Mitnick," said Mr. Kaplan with an expression that signified there is no accounting for human folly. "So now, fallow-students of beginnis' grate, to prezant de prazent, givink rizzons an' full description, ve vill hear fromm de *odder* member of de Boitday-Prazent-for-Mr.-Pockheel Committee!"

The loyal friends of Rose Mitnick cleaved the air

with their plaudits and turned toward their Guinevere. (Mr. Plonsky half-turned.)

But Miss Mitnick, skittish as a fawn under ordinary circumstances, now seemed totally indistinguishable from her background. She had slumped deep in her chair, her skin the color of oatmeal, her eyes stricken with panic.

"Mitnick," called Mr. Kaplan.

The wan maiden made a strangling sound; her lips were open but her tongue was paralyzed.

"*Mit*nick!" called Mr. Kaplan urgently.

Miss Mitnick had turned to stone.

"She got stage-fried!" cried Fanny Gidwitz.

"Svallowed her tong!" mourned Cookie Kipnis.

"Miss Mitnick, Miss Mitnick, stand op, Miss Mitnick!" moaned Mrs. Moskowitz. It had the cadence of a dirge.

"Somebody slep her hends!"

"Make 'Boo!' "

"Snep fingers!"

"Could be her shoes are too tight," ventured Mr. Blattberg, parading his *expertise*. "She nidds at lease a 5-B."

The hollow tones of Olga Tarnova rose above the others. "Wonce I saw octress, had seemilar choke-in-troat. Eight minutes. In Rossia. In weenter. By lohver's funeral. Was sod, sod." (Sometimes Mr. Parkhill thought Miss Tarnova could not so much as say "Good morning" without invoking some image of tragedy on the frozen steppes.)

Mr. Kaplan was staring at Miss Mitnick with as much horror as she was gaping at him with terror. "Mitnick," he called, pleading, "it's not for *me*. It's for

Mr. Pockheel!"

No other tocsin could have penetrated Miss Mitnick's benumbment. She rose, an automaton—ashen, trembling, clutching her handkerchief—fixed her eyes in a jellied glaze on a point in the middle of Mr. Parkhill's chest, and with muffled voice plunged into the fire: "On behalf of beginners' grade and all students in it, I presant this little key—" Miss Mitnick stopped "—this key—" she gibbered, blinking her eyelids. "Key... *key*..."

Mr. Kaplan snapped his fingers, reached into his pocket, and pulled out a red ribbon from which two tiny keys dangled. "*Two* keys," he whispered. "Make plural."

Miss Mitnick took the ribbon, held it out stiffly, and completed her ordeal: "I presant these *keys*, to now open the guaranteed genuine leather, full-lined, solid-bress-hinges—the case for Mr. Parkhill!"

Now it was done. Applause. Delight. Felicitations. A hush. They were all looking at Mr. Parkhill again.

He coughed. "Thank you. I—er—am very grateful. It's very kind of you, of all of you. Thank you ever so much." As he fitted one of the little keys into the lock, he noticed for the first time that the case was initialed. The initials were "M.P.". M. P.? How strange. "M.P." stood for "mounted police," or "Member of Parliament." But *his* initials were not M.P. His first name did not even begin with "M."

He heard the rain splattering on the window, and the distant city noises with their ubiquitous intimation of the raffish. At Tilsbury, the peepers would herald each spring in night-whistlings so constant and so melodious that none who first heard them could believe his ears. For some reason Mr. Parkhill suddenly recalled the odd expression on Mr. Linton's face that time he had first told him about the American Night Preparatory School for Adults. Then Aunt Agatha's prim features materialized before him....

Mr. Parkhill looked up. The faces that loomed before him were rather larger than life, it seemed: Mr. Kaplan, Miss Mitnick, Miss Tarnova...Pinsky, Plonsky, Caravello....They seemed unified, for once, in most unfamiliar concord.

And it was clear to him, of a sudden, why the initials on the case were "M.P." Obviously. *They* always called him "Mr. Parkhill." What reason was there, indeed, to use his first name? Why, he could hardly remember the last time anyone had addressed him by it.

Mr. K*A*P*L*A*N *Bares His Teeth*

Mr. Parkhill was concerned about "v"s and "w"s. For weeks he had known that something would have to be done about them—something drastic. For of all the peculiar and haphazard phonetics through which his pupils mangled the English language, their blithe miscegenation of "v"s and "w"s was perhaps the most annoying.

He could understand the ancient habits that converted the long "e" into the short "i," or transformed the broad "a" into the clipped "e." He could even accept the powerful linguistic momentum that made so simple and straightforward a syllable as "six," for example, emerge from the larynxes of his fledglings as "sick" (Mr. Scymzak), "sex" (Miss Tarnova), "sox" (Mr. Matsoukas), and "seex" (Mr. Marcus). But the ad libitum interchange of "v"s for "w"s and "w"s for "v"s —that seemed quite unnecessary.

Mr. Parkhill had discussed the problem, during a recess, with Miss Higby, of Composition, Grammar, and Civics. And Miss Higby had agreed without hesitation that no speech imperfection caused *her* so much anxiety, either, as "the voiced fricative and labiodental consonants." That was just the way she put it. (Miss Higby had an M.A. in education from Teachers College.)

"They just don't seem to be interested in mastering their 'w's," Mr. Parkhill had said earnestly.

"Nor their '*v*'s, Mr. Parkhill! Let's not gloss over their 'v's!" Miss Higby seemed quite emphatic about it.

"I—don't," said Mr. Parkhill.

There was a pause.

"Drill, drill, drill!" said Miss Higby suddenly.

"I beg your pardon?"

"I said, 'Drill, drill, drill.' *That's* the way to stamp out the careless enunciation of 'v's and 'w's."

"Oh."

A sacrificial gleam invaded Miss Higby's eyes. "I shall set aside ten minutes a night, *each* night, for nothing but 'v-w' drill!" When she raised her head that way, Miss Higby bore a certain resemblance to Joan of Arc—a slightly stout and Gaelic Joan of Arc. "Their 'v's and 'w's *must* improve!"

"Yes," Mr. Parkhill admitted. "They must."

"I know that Mr. Krout works very hard on 't's and 'th's in *his* class."

"Yes," Mr. Parkhill said, "he does."

"And Mr. Robinson is greatly concerned about the way our students say 'jomp' for 'jump' and 'goil' for 'girl.' "

"Oh," said Mr. Parkhill.

Miss Higby looked him straight in the eye, lowering her voice. "I think you will agree, Mr. Parkhill, that it is in the beginners' grade that proper speech habits can best be inculcated. If you would—"

The bell rang.

"Yes," said Mr. Parkhill quickly, "I shall."

He wished Miss Higby would be a little less militant

about things.

Mr. Parkhill was not a severe disciplinarian, but he rather prided himself on the fact that, once duty set a given course, there were no bounds to his perseverance. When, accordingly, the opportunity presented itself to take the enunciation of "v"s and "w"s by the horns, Mr. Parkhill did not falter.

The opportunity came during an exercise in vocabulary, when Mr. Kaplan, asked to give a sentence containing the word "value," replied, "Vell, ven ve walue somting, ve villink—"

"*Mr.* Kaplan!"

Mr. Kaplan stopped dead in his vocal tracks. "I didn't finished." His tone was injured.

"I know. You didn't fin*ish*, not you 'didn't fin*ished*.' But your *enunciation*, Mr. Kaplan."

Dismay crept into Mr. Kaplan's left eye. "Vas *wronk* mine santence mit 'walue'?"

"N-no," Mr. Parkhill said warily. "But your 'v's and 'w's, Mr. Kaplan. You did not pronounce a single one of your 'v's or 'w's correctly!"

Mr. Kaplan murmured "Oh," sadly.

"What you said was—er—something like this." Mr. Parkhill cleared his throat. " '*V*en *ve w*alue—' and so on. You pronounced the 'w's as if they were 'v's, and the 'v' as if it were a 'w'!"

Mr. Kaplan pondered Mr. Parkhill's comment ruefully. "You right, Mr. Pockheel. Mine dobble-youss is tarrible, an' mine 'v's is a shame. Still, I'll try to awoid mistakes—'

" '*A*void!' " Mr. Parkhill interpolated firmly. "There it is again."

Mr. Kaplan shook his head in despair. "Gattink voise

109

an' voise."

" '*W*orse and *w*orse!' " exclaimed Mr. Parkhill, the faint edge of desperation stealing into his voice. "Class, do you see what I mean?"

The class had no doubts whatsoever about what Mr. Parkhill meant. Few among them felt less culpable, vis-à-vis the vexing "v"s and "w"s, than Mr. Kaplan. Sighs of guilt, borne on winds of comprehension, scudded across the room.

"By me is a 'v' like a knife in mout!" confessed Mr. Pinsky.

"To me are 'w's like teffy-epples," mourned Shirley Ziev, who was once more bereft of her diamond ring.

Mrs. Moskowitz's moan was more explicit, and a good deal more grammatical, than any words she might have mustered to convey the vastness of her linguistic sins.

"Now, class," Mr. Parkhill said, "I know it seems difficult, but it is far, far from impossible. The 'v' and 'w' sounds are really quite simple, and *very* important. I might even say that for your purposes they are the most important of all the consonants. Even though you may enunciate every single vowel correctly, if you don't—"

"What's vowels?" asked Gus Matsoukas. He looked suspicious.

Mr. Parkhill studied the ceiling. "Mr. Matsoukas, don't you remember our lesson on vowels and consonants—?"

"No," said Mr. Matsoukas flatly.

Mr. Parkhill debated his next move. He wished Mr. Matsoukas were a bit more attentive. "Well, we haven't time to go into vowels and consonants thoroughly again, but just to touch on the highlights—'a,' 'e,' 'i,' 'o,' 'u,' and sometimes 'y,' are vowels. All the other letters in the alphabet are called *con*-sonants."

"What's consonants?" asked Mr. Matsoukas.

Mr. Parkhill looked at the floor. "All the letters *except* 'a,' 'e,' 'i,' 'o,' 'u,' and sometimes 'y.'"

"Why 'y' is only sometime?" asked Socrates' heir.

"Because sometimes 'y' is used as a vowel."

Mr. Matsoukas, who had a baffling way of changing horses in midstream, declared that he had always thought "consonants" were what you had in a friend.

"That," said Mr. Parkhill, "is 'con*fi*dence'!"

This only confused Mr. Matsoukas, who growled.

"Mein Gott, Matsoukas," cried Mr. Kaplan, "you ken give a titcher hot-failer."

"*I* don't say 'awoid'!" sneered proud Matsoukas.

"You *avoid* 'awoid,'" charged Mr. Kaplan, "vhich vas mine void an' not yours!"

"'*Whi*ch…*w*as…my *w*ord'!" said Mr. Parkhill. "You *must* correct that, Mr. Kaplan. I think it best that we all have a drill on 'v's and 'w's right now."

"Oooh," crooned Miss Tarnova.

"I'm raddy," sang out Mr. Pinsky. "I'm villink to—"

"Mistake!" Mr. Blattberg interjected. "That's just vat teacher means."

"'*What* teacher means,'" said Mr. Parkhill.

Mr. Kaplan gazed upon Mr. Blattberg with contempt. "Som corractor. Makink identical de mistake he's hollerink abot!"

Mr. Parkhill tapped on the desk firmly. He was beginning to feel alarmed. He was beginning to wish he had never consulted Miss Higby. "Let us put away our notebooks." His apprentices cleared the arms of their chairs of notebooks with a swoop. "And our pens and pencils." They put pens and pencils into storage. (Mr.

Kaplan, who attached some deep symbolic importance to his pencil, put his behind his ear.) "And books." Copies of *English for Beginners* thumped on the floor.

"Now, please. Everybody watch my lips." Mr. Parkhill wet his lips. (Mr. Plonsky rose, leaning forward, the better to see.) "First, I shall pronounce the 'v' sound."

A hush gripped his yeomen as Mr. Parkhill opened his mouth, put his upper teeth on and overlapping his lower lip, took a deep breath, and was just about to emit a long, firm "vvvv" when a sneeze from Peter Studniczka punctured the silence.

Mr. Parkhill closed his mouth.

"'Scooz," Mr. Studniczka mumbled miserably, and fumbled with his tie.

"That's quite all right." Mr. Parkhill was careful to smile. Mr. Studniczka was a sensitive soul. "Again, class. Notice. I place my upper teeth"—he tapped his upper teeth—"on my lower lip"—he tapped his lower lip—"and push my breath out to say—"

Mr. Studniczka sneezed again. "'Scooz." He was choked with shame.

"Er—surely." Mr. Parkhill cleared his throat. "Watch my lips now. Ready…"

"Studniczka! Hold beck!" cried Mr. Kaplan.

Mr. Parkhill withdrew his teeth from their perch on and overlapping his lower lip and went to the blackboard. It might be wiser to start the drill with the "w" sound. He took a piece of chalk and printed: "WE."

"'We,'" said Mr. Parkhill. "A very common word. Let us try the 'w' sound." (The class accepted this *volte-face* without protest.) "Notice, please. I shall round my lips this way—" Mr. Parkhill's lips contracted into a perfect zero—"and say 'ooo.'" He said "Oooo…"

The class was enchanted.

"Now, will you all do that, please? Everyone. Round lips..."

Thirty-odd students puckered sixty-odd lips to round thirty-odd mouths. They looked as if they had swallowed alum.

"Now, *without moving your lips*, simply expel your breath and say 'oooo'!"

Not a single lip moved as a mass explosion of air through rounded mouths formed a prolonged and melodious "*Ooooooo...*"

"Good! Now I shall say '*eeee*'—watch, please—like this." Mr. Parkhill drew his lips far apart, clenched his teeth with unintentional ferocity, and said "*Eeeee.*"

The beginners' grade had never been so fascinated. They bared their teeth, falling into leers of variant ferocity, and gave forth a mistral of eerie "*Eeeeee...*"s.

"Splendid!" said Mr. Parkhill. "Let's take the 'oooo' again. Round mouths...firm lips...expel..."

"Oooo," moaned the resolute pupils.

"Excellent! Now—lips apart, teeth together..."

"Eeee..."wailed the steadfast scholars.

"Perfect! Now let's put the sounds in order—this way." Mr. Parkhill rounded his lips. " 'Oooo.' " He bared his teeth. " 'Eeee.' " He repeated the labial calisthenics. " 'Ooooo'...and 'eeeee.' "

The thrill of the chase spurred them on as they echoed: " 'Ooooo... eeee...' "

"And *now*," said Mr. Parkhill eagerly, "we put the two sounds closer, thus: 'Oooo–eeee...'."

The brave battalion crooned "Oooo–eeee."

"And if we now *join* the two sounds, this way—'oo-ee,' 'oo-ee'..."—his loyal lieutenants joined the two

113

sounds with mounting excitement—"we will have pronounced an absolutely perfect 'WE'!"

"Hoorah!"

"I did it!"

"You *hoid*?!"

They were beside themselves with joy—grinning, chortling, reeling on the heights of achievement. They *had*, without knowing it, pronounced perfect "w"s. They had wrung the secret, the baffling and elusive secret, from the voiced labial open consonant, which need never again hold terror for them.

Mr. Parkhill was delighted. "We," he repeated gaily. "We…"

"Oo-ee! Oo-ee!" sang Miss Goldberg, and rewarded herself with a nougat.

"Oo-ee… oo-ee…oo-ee!" wheed Oscar Trabish, like a tippler on New Year's Eve.

"Fine!" said Mr. Parkhill.

"Wohnderful," cooed Miss Tarnova.

"Look!" laughed Mr. Pinsky. "Ooee, ooee. All of a certain, I can do!"

"Mr. Pockheel is a ginius!" rhapsodized Mr. Kaplan.

All over the room students faced each other, rounding their lips, baring their teeth, pronouncing mellifluous "Ooo-eee"s. (Mr. Plonsky faced left, unaware that Miss Gursky, who always sat there, was missing tonight, and hurled his triumphant "Ooo-ee"s into an uninhabited sector.)

"*Ex*cellent!" Mr. Parkhill's pleasure was exceeded only by his pride. "You *see* how simple it is? Now precisely the same use of your lips will pronounce perfect 'w's in any word. Let's try some others." He printed a challenging "WERE" on the blackboard.

"Just the same way, class. First, 'ooo'...then 'er'—and together, 'ooo-er'—which becomes 'were.' All together..."

"Ooooo-*er*" came back to him in one lusty gust. "Were!"

"Ooooo-*ait*," called Mr. Parkhill. "Wait!"

"Ooooo-ait. Wait!"

"Ooooo-ish, *wish*."

"Ooooo-ish," they echoed ghostily, "wish!"

"Will...warm...woman..." The words rolled out with fervor. "Want...what...wake..." Strong "Ooooo"s began each word; teeth flashed as lips flew back—and another word beginning with "w" whirled toward the stars.

"Why! Won! Wealth!" How proudly their voices rang.

"Now let's try a whole sentence," said Mr. Parkhill, carried away by success. The first part of the sentence he wrote on the board was a stab in the dark—but the second was sheer inspiration:

> While we were waiting with William West,
> we were wondering where Walter White was.

"My!" cried Mr. Kaplan in admiration.

"Isa plenty 'w's!" said Miss Caravello. (Miss Caravello tended to be literal-minded.)

"Planty? Ha! *All!* If Mr. Pockheel gives dobble-youss, he gives *dobble*-youss!"

"Oy," moaned Mrs. Moskowitz.

Mr. Parkhill tapped on the desk. "Let's try the whole sentence, class. Take it slowly. Remember to round your mouths." He felt the special exhilaration of those who lead pilgrims to Mecca. "Miss Kipnis, suppose you read the sentence first."

Miss Kipnis swallowed nervously, rose, and reconnoitred the sentence sprayed with "w"s like an Indian scout well trained in ambuscades. "Oo–ile oo–ee oo–ere oo–aiting…" Miss Kipnis maneuvered her mouth around the fourteen "w"s with fear and trembling, but not a single error.

"Cookie!" cried Miss Shimmelfarb.

"T'ree chiss fa Kipnis!" exclaimed Mr. Kaplan.

Miss Kipnis sat down, trailing unfamiliar clouds of glory.

"*Splen*did!" Mr. Parkhill said. "Next—"

Mr. Kaplan was waving his hand furiously. "Miss Tarnova."

Mr. Kaplan's hand went down; Miss Tarnova stood up. For a moment she looked as though she might sit down again, so pale was she before the fearful stretches of "While we were waiting with William West, we were wondering where Walter White was." She faltered, "Perhahps I fail…" but Hyman Kaplan sounded a ringing call to the colors: "Remamber Kipnis!"

Miss Tarnova fluttered her languorous lashes, sniffed at her perfumed handkerchief, rounded her cherry lips, and fell upon the "w"-resplendent sentence like a Cossack upon a Turk. Nary a voiced fricative marred the perfect parade of "w"s that issued from Olga Tarnova's circular lips.

"Excellent!" exclaimed Mr. Parkhill.

"Hau Kay," shrugged Hyman Kaplan. (Apparently Olga Tarnova did not deserve "t'ree chiss": she had shown cowardice under fire.)

"Next—" Mr. Parkhill glanced around the room.

Everyone wanted to be next. The upraised hands were a forest, darkening the air. Eyes burned with ardor, cheeks flushed with hope at the chance to vanquish the dread "w" that had at last been brought to bay.

" Er—"

Mr. Kaplan's hand was waving in frenzy. "Mr. Pockheel! Mr. Pockheel!" The man looked as if he would burst right there and then if denied his moment in the sun.

"Mr. Kaplan."

He rose, luminous. "Hau boy!"

"Er—Mr. Kaplan," Mr. Parkhill said diplomatically. "Please be careful. Speak slowly, and remember, keep your lips absolutely round!"

Mr. Kaplan nodded. "Arond itch single dobble-you mine mot is goink to make a detour! 'Oooooo' den 'eeee' ...Hau Kay!" He flung his head back and charged. "Ooooo-ile! Ooooo-ee! Ooooo-ere! Ooooo-aiting..." Tension gripped the class. "Ooooo-ith ooooo-illiam ooooo-est—"

"*Good*, Mr. Kaplan."

"—ooo-ee ooo-ere ooo-ondering ooo-ere ooo-alter ooo-ite ooo-as!"

"Perfect, Mr. Kaplan!"

"*Bella, bella!*"

Mr. Pinsky broke into applause.

Miss Mitnick gave Mr. Kaplan an adulatory smile.

Miss Tarnova lamented, "*Any*won can speak porfect now...."

"You see, class?" Mr. Parkhill observed happily. "That's all there is to it. Now, if you will only practice—"

"Prectice?" Mr. Kaplan's voice rang out. "Fromm nah on, ve vill voik vit dobble-youss till ve vouldn't iven vhisper—"

Mr. Parkhill did not hear the rest of Mr. Kaplan's gallant pledge. Mr. Parkhill did not even see Mr.

117

Kaplan. Darkness had fallen before his eyes.

Mr. K*A*P*L*A*N *Answers an Ad*

It had seemed such a good idea at the time. Indeed, Mr. Parkhill was rather proud of it. After all, his students were adults, not children; and as adults they could be expected to respond with deeper interest, keener enthusiasm, to assignments they could put to practical use. It was with a feeling of genuine constructiveness, therefore, that Mr. Parkhill had announced: "Your homework, class, will be of special interest, I believe." He smiled.

Mr. Parkhill found himself smiling a great deal lately—not because he was a smiling type (on the contrary, he was, *au fond*, an earnest or unsmiling type), and not because he actually felt like smiling. He smiled a great deal because he knew that his students expected it of him. It helped their morale. He could not help but see that they reacted to his every mood—elated by his approval, depressed by the faintest inkling of his displeasure.

Nor could Mr. Parkhill blame them. He knew how nettlesome is English as a language, how difficult to teach, how painful to master. He could understand his fledglings' seizing any clue or cue or crutch to aid them in the long, hard climb to comprehension. "The

119

assignment," he continued, the smile fastened to his lips, "is a *practical* exercise which you will, I trust, be able to put to er—practical use."

At the first "practical" his proselytes sat up; at the second, they leaned forward. If there was anything they yearned for, it was to wring some semblance of utility from a heartless tongue.

"Select an advertisement out of a newspaper and answer it!" Mr. Parkhill paused cheerfully. His cheer changed to doubt; for to his surprise, not jubilance but apprehension sprang into their once eager faces.

"Answer an *att*?" someone queried.

"What kind?" someone quavered.

"From vhere?" someone quaked.

"Now, now," said Mr. Parkhill in a soothing tone, "the assignment is not that difficult. After all, you have all seen the 'Help Wanted' or 'For Sale' columns in the newspapers." He replaced his ailing smile with a fresh edition. "Well, simply look through a newspaper, select an ad, *any* ad that interests you, and—er—answer it!"

The alarums of anxiety were superseded by groans of dismay, and climaxed by an "Oy!" of unmistakable defeat. That was Mrs. Moskowitz, already fanning herself with her notebook.

"Remember, class," Mr. Parkhill pressed on, refusing to be discouraged, "we have had exercises in writing letters before—both personal and business. Let's say this homework involves simply *another* exercise in letter writing."

"Ufcawss! Plain an' tsimple! Jost anodder latter!" That was Hyman Kaplan, and for once Mr. Parkhill felt grateful for that dauntless spirit, that unquenchable fire.

"Are there any questions?"

Miss Goldie Pomeranz raised her hand. (Actually, Miss Pomeranz, a diffident scholar, raised only one finger of her hand.) "Could you be so kind to give a for instance?"

"I beg your pardon?"

"She means, be so kind and give an example," said Miss Mitnick helpfully.

"Ha!" scoffed Mr. Kaplan. "Who nidds exemples? Mr. Pockheel's axplainink is poifick! Iven a baby could unnistand!" He seared Miss Pomeranz with a glare, for flinching before what any baby could master, and froze Miss Mitnick with a frown, for serving as accessory to the crime of perfidious Pomeranz.

"I only tried to help Miss Pomeranz," explained Miss Mitnick plaintively.

"An' *I*," said Mr. Kaplan, "don't nidd exemples!"

"Look who's talking!" exclaimed Mr. Plonsky, looking by error at Mr. Studniczka, who had not uttered a sound.

"Edgar Ellen Kaplen," sneered Mr. Blattberg, twirling his gold chain with bravado.

"Gentlemen," said Mr. Parkhill hastily, "Miss Pomeranz's request is quite in order. I shall be glad to—er—offer several examples." The Mitnick-Plonsky-Blattberg task force basked in Mr. Parkhill's favor. "You may, for instance, answer an ad that offers to rent a room, or sell a car, or—" To his acute distress, Mr. Parkhill's mind suddenly went blank; he scoured the cellars of memory for those images, those classified images, he knew must be stored there—by the thousands. Memory failed him not. "Or take a free dancing lesson!"

"*Dencing* lessons?" echoed Mrs. Moskowitz in astonishment. "By my age who takes from Arthur Murphy?"

"It's only vun *exemple*!" blurted Mr. Kaplan. "Mr. Pockheel also offert a room—"

"My flet has already four rooms, so who needs—"

"So don't rant a room! Buy a car!"

"A car?" sputtered Gus Matsoukas. "Who affords?"

"*Buy it sacondhend*!"

"Class—"

"An exemple isn't a pair hencuffs!" cried Mr. Kaplan, showering more succor on Mr. Parkhill than he either required or desired. "Matsoukas, you got to use imegination!"

"Ads are full little words," complained Mrs. Rodriguez with feeling. (Mrs. Rodriguez was the proprietress of a grocery store in East Harlem.)

"Those," said Mr. Parkhill at once, "are *abbreviations*—and working with them might turn out be one of the most useful features of the assignment."

"I no unnastan' 'brevyations,'" declared Miss Caravello.

Mr. Kaplan hurled a "Ha!" at craven Caravello. "Abbrevyations didn't bodder Colombiss, Judge Vashington—"

"They dida not answera ad!"

"Dey vould denk Gott for de chence!" the invincible advocate declaimed. "To find a varm room, instad cold vilderness! To go by car, instad on blidding fitt—"

"Mr. Kap—"

"Stop!" roared Mr. Plonsky, groping through an outrage that only reblurred his vision. "How you drag in by his heels Colombus? Where Colombus used abbreviation?"

"That's right!"

"Vhere?"

"Give even one case!"

"Keplen," said Mr. Kaplan with hauteur, "is discossink a sobjeck, not takink a cross-exemination!"

Mr. Pinsky cried "Psssh!" and slapped his cheek.

Mr. Plonsky smote his forehead and groaned.

"That will be enough, class," said Mr. Parkhill crossly. "There are many *simple* ads from which you may choose. I suggest you copy the one you decide to answer, or clip it out of the paper, and bring it to class with your letter. I am quite sure——"

Before he could tell them what he was quite sure of, Mr Kaplan's simmering contempt came to a boil. "Vat kind students ve got in cless enyhow? Did Mr. Pockheel bag us on banded knees to comm to school? Did he sand ot ingraved inwitations? Did de Prazident sign a law averybody got to enswer an ed or dey'll die in Elcatraz?"

This indignant list of particulars roused the partisans, who raised a fearful furore—louder than Mr. Parkhill's tapping pointer, drowning out his familiar abjurations.

Mr. Pinsky accused Mrs. Rodriguez of jeopardizing the class's entire future by questioning Mr. Parkhill's judgment; Miss Caravello raged that Mr. Pinsky was no more than a lackey to Mr. Kaplan's every whim.

Miss Gidwitz declaimed that Mr. Kaplan was an adornment to the grade and a model for the brave; Miss Tarnova fumed that Mr. Kaplan was a wolf in "ship's clothes" who fomented discord among the innocent. Mr. Plonsky excoriated those "stoogies" who blindly followed where e'er blind Kaplan led (a most telling metaphor, considering the source); Miss Kipnis blasted Mr. Plonsky for attacking the pygmies on the sidelines

123

when Gulliver himself waited on the field of honor.

Miss Goldberg reached for a peppermint. Mrs. Tomasic crossed herself.

"America is free country!" shouted Mr. Scymzak in a burst of patriotism.

"Amarica," thundered Hyman Kaplan, "did not gat free fromm pipple afrait to enswer an ed!"

But all that was long over and done with. Now it was nine-fifteen, the following Monday night. All was peaceful, placid. The blackboards were crammed with homework.

The assignment had turned out far better than Mr. Parkhill had dared to hope. Miss Kipnis had opened the evening with a rather effective, if redundant, reply to an advertisement of the Bell Telephone Company:

Dear Telephone Co.
   You want young women. I am young woman.
You print "salary good." Good.
   You want girls to come to office Wed. 9—1.
I will come to office Wed. 9—1.
                    Happily yours,
             Clara (Cookie) Kipnis, "Miss"

The diagnosis of this offering had been brisk and pointed.

Mr. Matsoukas had questioned the propriety of the salutation, "Dear Telephone Co.," suggesting that "Dear Company" would be better.

Miss Ziev remarked that placing a "Miss" between quotation marks was both misleading and gratuitous (Miss Ziev's left hand was once more adorned by the ring with which Mr. Andrassy had re-sworn eternal devotion), since "a Miss is a Miss, so put in front like a Mrs."

Miss Mitnick opined that "Happily yours" was not proper in business correspondence, and might, besides, give the Bell Telephone System the impression that the applicant was too flighty to be entrusted with "calls from a long distance."

Mrs. Yanoff wondered whether it was not more accurate to write "I will come to office *between* 9 and 1," instead of "I will come to office 9–1." "The way *she* wrote," observed the sage in black, "she will be standing on her lags four hours."

Mr. Wilkomirski had followed Miss Kipnis; and Stanislaus Wilkomirski, Mr. Parkhill was delighted to see, had triumphed over fear. He had selected an advertisement for "go-getters" interested in augmenting their income by selling, on commission, hand-colored portraits of the Pope which were "guaranteed to sell like hot cakes." Mr. Wilkomirski's salutation was correct, his text commendable, his final greeting impeccable. His downfall, alas, came via an entirely unnecessary postscript:

p.s. I also like to sell hot cakes.

Mr. Parkhill went to considerable pains to explain the difference between selling hot cakes and selling *like* hot cakes, and hastened on.

Not all the students, of course, had reached the laudable levels of a Kipnis or a Wilkomirski. Mr. Scymzak, for instance, had answered a notice announcing the sale of "Furn., unpainted" by declaring that he was a wizard at removing paint from furnaces. Miss

Shimmelfarb had unfortunately mistaken "Lab. Tech." for "labor teacher." Mr. Guttman had applied for a position which required "Highest refs." by stating that he heartily approved of any business concern that gave "highest refunds."

And there had been other pitfalls which no one, not even Mr. Parkhill, could possibly have foreseen. Mrs. Rodriguez had replied to a notice offering $25 reward for a lost dog with a buoyant letter that contained this baffling codicil:

> Send $25.00. I found your college dog.

At this point, the class might have gotten entirely out of hand ("What kind dog is smot enough to pess even high school?" "They lost a dog, not a student!") had not Mr. Parkhill, in a flash of inspiration, solved the mystery: Mrs. Rodriguez had simply thought "Collie" the abbreviation for "college."

Tiny Mrs. Tomasic had drafted an answer to "Wanted: Housekeeper" which cunningly reduced the probability of error to the very bone:

> Dear Ad:
> I am housekeeper.
> Mrs. F. Tomasic

There was not much one could do with *that* kind of homework.

Now the last platoon was at the blackboard. Rochelle Goldberg was putting the finishing touches to her *précis* for the post of receptionist for Juno Princess Slips. Mr. Pinsky was completing an epistle to "Zig Zag Zippers,

Inc." Miss Olga Tarnova, whose superior manner more than ever hinted of a time when spurned lovers had flung themselves off cliffs from Monte Carlo to Murmansk, was addressing some Hindu seer who claimed to have direct entrée to the hereafter:

> Ahmed Taj' Chandra
> Box 308
> Eve. Post
> Ah, dear Ahmed
> I have seen soulful ad you wrote to help menkind grow in Secret Powers. Many nights I sleep awake—

Mr. Parkhill read no further; he *wished* Miss Tarnova would choose less exotic material.

The letter to Miss Tarnova's right was Mr. Kaplan's. There could be no doubt whatsoever that it was Mr. Kaplan's, for on the board was printed:

ANSWERING AN AD
by
H✳Y✳M✳A✳N K✳A✳P✳L✳A✳N

The man who had placed this flamboyant heading on the austere slate was poised before his handiwork as if he were Rembrandt—one hand holding his notebook as if it were a palette, the other wielding the chalk as if it were a brush, examining his masterpiece with narrowed eyes and a lilting hum of approbation, taking a step back, or a step forward, as the divine afflatus moved him. Mr. Kaplan *loved* working at the blackboard: To him it was no lifeless surface on which to record the prosaic; to him it was a golden portal through which to reach posterity.

As Miss Tarnova signed her name to her letter with a flourish, the many bracelets on her wrist tinkling, the master, rudely jarred out of inspiration, scowled, "Tarnova, eider take off or tune op your musical instruments!"

Miss Tarnova did not deign response; she merely flared her fine nostrils and drifted back to her seat, a Grand Duchess addressed by a peasant.

"Please finish now," Mr. Parkhill quickly called. "Good…Take your seats….We shall begin with—Miss Goldberg."

It was a happy choice. Miss Goldberg had outdone herself. Her application for the post of receptionist at Juno Princess Slips was terse and telling. The only question anyone raised was whether "Dear Madam" might not be more fitting than "Dear Gentlemen" for "someone in princess slips."

Mr. Pinsky's letter, to Zig Zag Zippers, Inc., ran into stormier weather. Mr. Pinsky had for some reason composed his entire communication in capitals, thusly:

> HELLO.
> I SAW YOUR AD FOR BUS OPERATER.
> I ACCEPT $10,000, SO—

"Holy smoky!" Mr. Wilkomirski, ever the sexton, exclaimed before the floor was even thrown open for discussion. "That is telegram, not letter!"

"Is this night school or Western Union?" demanded Mr. Blattberg.

Mr. Kaplan rushed to the aid of his aide-de-camp. "Telegrems gat rizzolts! Congradulation, Pinsky!"

Mr. Plonsky raised his hand, peered at Miss

Pomeranz, whom he mistook for Mr. Pinsky, and in mordant tone asked whether any business in its right mind would offer ten thousand dollars in wages to a bus driver. "Not even in Tel Aviv!"

The challenge did not faze Sam Pinsky, who, with a confident smile, handed Mr. Parkhill the very newspaper clipping he had elected to answer. The ten thousand dollars was there, all right, but it had been requested, not offered: Mr. Pinsky looked badly shaken when Mr. Parkhill explained that "Bus. opp." meant "business opportunity" and not "bus operator."

"Don't take it hod," Mr. Kaplan murmured.

Miss Tarnova read her letter next, her hand at her throat. "Ah, dear Ahmed," intoned the exiled child of the steppes, "I hahve seen souful ad you wrote, to help menkind grow in secret power..." (Mrs. Moskowitz yawned; even the lure of the East made scant impression on Mrs. Moskowitz; she had enough trouble keeping awake during Open Questions, much less attuning her soul to the supernatural.) "Many nights I sleep awake—"

"You slip *avake*?" cried Mr. Kaplan. "Maybe you also sit stendink op?"

Olga Tarnova sailed on across her sea of limitless woe. And when her dulcet reading was finished, Mr. Parkhill said, "Very good, Miss Tarnova." (Mr. Kaplan's face fell.) "That is a most *interesting* letter. There are—er—a few mistakes, but on the whole you have improved in every way." And she *had* improved; one had but to recall Miss Tarnova's memorable recitation: "Leopold Stokowski, Don't Butcher Tschaikowski!"

Mr. Parkhill threw the floor open to discussion.

The class conducted it with decorum: Mr. Mat-soukas recommended a comma after the unpunctuated salutation; Mrs. Yanoff persuaded Miss Tarnova to *lie* awake instead of sleeping awake; Mr. Scymzak intimated that although "men" was the plural of "man," "menkind" was not necessarily the plural of "mankind."

Miss Mitnick addressed herself to Miss Tarnova's final greeting:

> I remain,
> A soul–mat
> Olga Tarnova

"I'm sure," Miss Mitnick said diplomatically, "Miss Tarnova intanded to put 'e' on the end of 'mat.' "

But as Mr. Parkhill started to convert the "mat" of Miss Tarnova's soul into its "mate," Mr. Kaplan put in sternly, "Podden me, are ve corractink *intands* or ectuals? Tarnova wrote don 'soul—mat.' "

"In world of spirit," flared Miss Tarnova, "we are all taking new names!"

"For dat you don't nidd de voild of spirits! In Sing Sing are planty pipple who took new names!"

"*Bodzye moy!*" cursed Miss Tarnova, and sniffed at a scent from Araby.

"Next," said Mr. Parkhill quickly, glancing at the clock. Only five minutes were left. He had hoped, somehow, that there would be less.

The room stirred, a field of wheat before a heralding wind, as Mr. Kaplan rose. He rose in the manner of Disraeli, about to inform an admiring House that India was now England's own. A careless smile, a shooting of the cuffs, a charitable glance for those unequal to what lay ahead, then Hyman Kaplan grasped his lapels in the finest parliamentary fashion and, in a voice of limpid timbre, read: " 'Enswerink an ed, by Hyman Keplen.' "

Mr. Parkhill lowered himself glumly into his chair. In his mind, Henley's *Invictus* stirred.

Mr. Kaplan's text, which he read with measured weight and matchless fervor, ran:

> Box 701
> Daily New
> N.Y.

Dear Box,

One day was Hyman Kaplan home, feeling blues, thinking What is world coming to? No body happy, people worryd, we live on vulcano.

"How a man can find peace?" asked Hyman Kaplan. How a man can escape this jongle? No way.

No way? Stop, *Hyman Kaplan*! Look. Listen. Read what is here in front your eyes! A wonderful ad. What it says? This it says—

> "Man with ambition. Must have ideas, imag., init., drive. Salary no object.
> Box 701."

Box 701, look no farther! I am that man.
1) Ideas.   I have plenty ideas.
2) Imag.   I can imagine anything.
3) Init.   Initials are H.K.
4) Drive. I don't, but am willing to learn.
                                                    V.T.Y.

H＊Y＊M＊A＊N K＊A＊P＊L＊A＊N

Before Mr. Kaplan had even finished reading, the hounds were barking at his heels.

"What kind cuckoo is that 'Dear Box'?" glared Mr. Plonsky through the fiercer lens of his bifocals.

"*Important* eds give only 'Box,'" replied Mr. Kaplan.

"Should be 'Dear *sir*,'" said Miss Mitnick.

"How you know is only vun man in their box?" rejoined Mr. Kaplan.

"You were feeling 'blues'?" blustered Mr. Blattberg. "Should be singular —'*blue*'!"

"I falt *vary* blue! Plural."

"'Daily *New*' should be 'Daily News'!" protested Stanislaus Wilkomirski.

"Since ven is vun copy plural?" snapped Mr. Kaplan, reversing his field.

"'Vulcano'? Spell wrong!" exclaimed Miss Caravello, and Mr. Kaplan made no demurrer. (Miss Caravello's years in Naples gave her a clear edge where the pyroclastic was concerned.)

Now the emendations came fast and furious.

"'No body' should be one 'nobody,'" trilled Mrs. Tomasic.

"'Drive' in ads means anergy," bristled Mr. Guttman, "not car-driving."

"What is that bandaged-op 'V.T.Y.'? Is Keplan too *weak* to write out?" Mr. Plonsky was so furious that he resorted to the gesture of supreme insult: he deliberately spun around in his chair and presented his back to both the blackboard and his *bête noire*.

Now they swarmed across the cornered warrior, wave upon wave, not heeding Mr. Parkhill's anxious calls for order, not pausing for Mr. Kaplan's rejoinders. Had they been less drunk with success they would have noticed that Mr. Kaplan was not even attempting a single rejoinder. Strangely enough, he was standing unperturbed, unruffled, regarding from the peak of dignity those who clamored for his blood. Such valor was too much for the faithful who always rallied to his banner.

"Keplen, *say* somthing!" begged steadfast Pinsky, mopping his pate.

"Mr. Kaplan, *answer*," pleaded loyal Gidwitz.

"Go on, Mr. Edison, make a miracle," sneered Mr. Plonsky, addressing the rear wall.

"Class…" Mr. Parkhill frowned crossly to still the mounting rancors. "We *must* speak one at a time! Those who wish to comment on Mr. Kaplan's letter will please wait to be recognized."

So ordained, the discussion turned more orderly, though no more merciful.

"I see five mistakes," said Miss Mitnick. "At least."

The mistakes she saw were but the beginning. Other voices sought Mr. Parkhill's sanction; other scholars leaped into the mêlée; the errata of Hyman Kaplan unrolled like an endless scroll.

Yet to every blunder pinpointed, and every change volunteered, Mr. Kaplan made not the slightest response. Mr. Parkhill placed correction after correction on the battle-scarred board, yet Mr. Kaplan offered not a word of protest or defense or elaboration. He simply stood there, lofty, courtly, neither chastened nor abashed. Mr. Parkhill even thought he caught a gleam of vanity in Mr. Kaplan's eye—for the very magnitude of the havoc he had wrought upon an ancient tongue. Once, he even tendered a little word of praise to colleagues so keen as to find so many errors in one brief

133

span of prose.

The longer Mr. Kaplan met criticism with such nobility, and rectification with such grace, the more uneasy Mr. Parkhill found himself becoming. He could understand composure under fire. He could even understand Mr. Kaplan's opacity to humiliation. But he did not for a moment doubt that in point of fact Mr. Kaplan was employing some new and secret stratagem, or had thrown a net of camouflage across some dark and unsprung trap.

Only a minute or two remained now, and almost nothing left to correct, when Miss Mitnick, sedately implacable, raised her hand yet once more. "Why Mr. Kaplan gives his initials? Doesn't the abbreviation 'i-n-i-t' mean 'initia*tive*'?"

"Very good," said Mr. Parkhill, admiring Miss Mitnick's acumen: he had not thought anyone would catch that. " 'Initiative,' Mr. Kaplan."

Mr. Kaplan nodded, polite but unpersuaded. "Dat ed *I* enswered vanted initials."

"Mr. Kaplan," frowned Mr. Parkhill, "there is hardly any—er—room for difference about what 'i-n-i-t' means."

"In ganeral, or in dis poticular ed?"

"Keplan, stop *sneaking*!" fumed Mr. Plonsky, covering his eyes.

"Edmit you wrong!" muttered Gus Matsoukas.

"Once only, *give* an inch!" pleaded Bessie Shimmelfarb.

Hyman Kaplan stood proud and silent.

"Mr. Kaplan," said Mr. Parkhill, "suppose we—er—refer to the ad's exact text."

"It's on de board."

"I have seen what is on the board," said Mr. Parkhill frigidly. "That is why I suggest we examine the actual copy of the actual ad—"

"Onfortunately," said Hyman Kaplan, "dere is no *ectual* copy...."

"Ha ha!" cried Mr. Plonsky, wheeling back to the front. "A trick!"

"No wohnder," crooned Miss Tarnova. "Batter admit....Tropped, tropped."

"He'sa caught at last!" Miss Caravello exulted. "*Che ha?*"

Mr. Kaplan surveyed them with sweet forbearance. "Vy should Keplen pay money to put de ed in a paper?"

There was a ghastly, beating moment as the monstrous truth dawned on some of them.

"Mr. Kaplan," wailed poor Miss Mitnick, "you mean *you made up the ad?*"

"Stop!" howled Mr. Plonsky, addressing not his blood-foe but the heartless gods.

Mr. Parkhill put his chalk down without a word. He did not even try to calm the maelstrom that swirled around him. Hyman Kaplan, never content with reality as he found it, had made up his own ad!

Perhaps it was his ungovernable need to be different. Perhaps it was his irrepressible urge to reconstruct life closer to his heart's desire. And perhaps, thought Mr. Parkhill with a shudder, the invincible, exasperating demon that found so happy a home in Hyman Kaplan's soul had known all along that there was no higher authority on earth for the meaning of "init." than the man who had put it into his own ad.

Mr Parkhill's Daymare

"A. Lincoln died. The poor slaves were no more bare-foot. Confaderats became citizens. So we put on their gravves flowers same as anyone. That is my virgin of Mem. Day."

That was the way Mrs. Rodriguez had concluded her contribution to the solemn day we commemorate on May 30.

Mr. Parkhill leaned back in his chair philosophically. At the last session of the class, two nights ago, he had given his neophytes a little lecture on Memorial Day, how Arlington Cemetery is its focus and the Unknown Soldier its shrine. His words had made a deeper impression than he would have imagined....

He started to correct Mrs. Rodriguez's homework, feeling rather relieved that she had written, rather than spoken, her heartfelt words. Had she, say during Recitation and Speech, *said* "virgin" for "version," Mr. Parkhill might not even have noticed it. But if he had...There would have been no problem in explaining "version" to his hardy flock; but "virgin"—! "Virgin," Mr. Parkhill could not help thinking, contained all sorts of dangers for the volatile personnel of the beginners' grade.

He turned to the next paper. It was by Rochelle Goldberg. On the first page was printed only this title:

Soldeirs and Sailors–Hurry!

Mr. Parkhill read it three times before insight came to his rescue; he gripped his red pencil and wrote across the page:

"Miss G.: You mean 'Hurrah!'—or even 'Hooray!' There is all the difference in the world between 'Hurrah' (or 'Hooray') and '*hurry*.' Consult your dictionary!"

He turned the page. To his surprise (now that he thought of it, the homework had been chock-full of surprises), a poem met his eyes:

I

Today remember
Last December
was no place
for Decoration Days

II

Soldeirs, sailors,
Airplaners, Marines
Shouldn't stand only
by hot-dog machines (like in Coney I.)

Who would have dreamed that beneath Rochelle Goldberg's plain exterior flowed such lyrical streams? He corrected the spelling of "soldeirs" and wrote "Good effort, Miss G." (He did not think it would help to comment on her meter.)

The next opus, a letter from Mr. Scymzak to someone addressed only as "Deer," contained this pearl:

In old times, armies went slow but today are speed.

At that moment Mr. Parkhill decided it was time to put his protégés through a vigorous drill on antonyms. That was one of the most useful by-products of homework; it not only revealed to Mr. Parkhill those areas in which his charges were weak; it also gave him time, away from the pressures of the classroom, to devise lessons specifically aimed at specific targets. "Antonyms!" he thought. "They are pretty shaky on their antonyms."

He opened the very next meeting of the class by announcing, "Tonight, class, we shall begin by brushing up on our opposites." (He would not, of course, dream of inflicting so bizarre a word as "antonyms" on his fledglings.) "Notebooks, please. Write five words in one column, and write their opposites—er—opposite." The innocent play on words pleased him. He could never understand why Miss Higby, according to all reports, conducted her class with such funereal rigor. "We shall then put our lists on the blackboard."

It was heartening to see how, with one accord, his students plunged into their work. Opposites seemed to enlist their enthusiasm—unlike irregular verbs, which they resented, or the subjunctive mood, which they loathed. Opposites were honest, open and above board. Confidence bloomed in the room.

Mr. Trabish unbuttoned his vest and sharpened his pencil happily. Miss Ziev set ball-point to paper *sans peur*. (The banns for Miss Ziev's alliance with Mr. Andrassy had officially been posted.) Mrs. Moskowitz even reversed a yawn in midstream, transforming torpidity to approval by a mere rerouting of breath. And Mr. Kaplan, a visionary gleam in his eye, cried, "Opposites! My!" He said it the way Dante might have uttered "Beatrice!" Then, with an avuncular beam toward Mr. Pinsky, he fell to.

It promised to be a fruitful evening. Mr. Parkhill strolled down the aisle, nodding to his followers, who smiled gratefully to their dominie. When he reached the back of the room, he lifted the window to let in the soft spring air, then strolled back, glancing at the notebooks in which opposites were sprouting like mushrooms.

After several minutes, Mr. Parkhill said, "One minute more, class," and in two minutes more called "Time...Will the following go to the board, please? Miss Mitnick...Mr. Guttman...Miss Shimmelfarb..." He called six names in all.

It was a confident platoon that advanced upon the blackboard, and a triumphant one that returned from its maneuvers. Their performance was a tribute to Mr. Parkhill's tutelage. Not a single mistake marred the quintet of antonyms Miss Mitnick had provided "happy...round...thin...lazy...hot." Only one lapse in spelling blemished Mr. Guttman's counterparts to "soft...dark...win...smart...pretty." Cookie Kipnis had tripped on the opposite of "wet," which she conceived of as "fry," and Mrs. Yanoff had somehow gotten the idea that the opposite of "country" is "jail." But all things considered, antonyms had gotten off to a flying start.

Mr. Parkhill sent six more scholars to the board. None turned in as faultless a performance as Miss Mitnick's, but none committed a *gaffe* as queer as Mrs. Yanoff's either.

He sent yet another sextette to the board. He felt quite cheerful, even optimistic. Nothing so warms the cockles of a teacher's heart as progress—visible, unmistakable progress—in his flock.

He smiled at the board. Mrs. Tomasic had neatly written, thus far:

> man — woman
> slow — fast
> hello — goodbye

Why, even wee Mrs. Tomasic was surpassing herself tonight.

Mr. Plonsky was printing, in the mammoth hand of the myopic:

> over — under
> save — spend
> strong — wick

Mr. Parkhill saw excellent possibilities in how he would approach the correcting of "wick."

He turned to Mr. Studniczka's offering. Poor Mr. Studniczka. Scowling, perspiring, he had flung himself against the pitiless battlements of English, only to fall back bloody and bruised:

> black — white
> white — black
> 1 — 2
> eat — not eat

Mr. Parkhill sighed. It was a long, hard row Peter

141

Studniczka had to hoe—but hoe it, Mr. Parkhill had no doubt, he would.

The next pupil at the board was Mr. Kaplan. Mr. Parkhill braced himself. After one glance at what Hyman Kaplan had conjured out of the unknown this time, he turned his back, and with bowed head sought the farthest corner of the room. *Frangas, non flectes.* What *could* one do about Mr. Kaplan? It was discouraging to confront such opacity to instruction.

Mr. Kaplan was standing before the board in absolute bliss, hand on hip, eyes transported, Cortes on a new peak in Darien. And he was humming—humming, just loud enough for everyone in the room to share his ecstasy, snatches of some triumphal hymn. It might have been from Lohengrin.

What induced such rapture in Mr. Kaplan's soul was (1) writing at the blackboard, which he loved; (2) anticipating the give-and-take of discussion, which he adored; (3) contemplating, with unabashed admiration, the wonders of his brain:

H*Y*M*A*N K*A*P*L*A*N
gives
5 Opp.

The name, as always, gleamed like a tri-colored pennant; the stars, as always, relieved the loneliness between one letter and another. Under his iridescent heading, the Ariel of the beginners' grade had written:

> Can Man live without Opp.? No! Why?
> Without opp. is impossible to discuss.
> Soppose someone says, "Wrong!" How you

can say "Right"? Only with opp.!

So Mr. Parkhill gives fine lesson—5 opp. So Hyman Kaplan presents:

Word	Opp.
1. Spic	Span
2. Tall	Shrimp
3.N. Caroline	S. Caroline

Mr. Parkhill dabbed at his brow with his handkerchief. It was going to be a difficult evening after all.

Several of the students, perusing Mr. Kaplan's work with that special, hawklike zeal they reserved for the thorn in their side, were exchanging expectant chortles. A cocksure grin sped from Mr. Plonsky to Mr. Blattberg; a knowing gloat winged back from Mr. Blattberg to Mr. Plonsky. Miss Tarnova moved an inscrutable smile along her inscrutable lips and honed her dagger for the carnage to come. Someone chortled.

"Quiet, please," said Mr. Parkhill mechanically. How often had he tried to *restrain* Mr. Kaplan, who approached the most routine assignments with exuberance. But he had never been able to hold that untamed imagination in leash. It was like asking a gladiator to strike only one blow, or a Magellan to traverse only one sea.

Once, in fulfilling an assignment Mr. Parkhill had most carefully circumscribed ("One page describing how you spent your weekend"), Mr. Kaplan had submitted no less than five pages on the role of leisure in a civilization racked by tension. Another time, in executing "Ten interrogative sentences ending with 'he—or she—asked,' " Mr. Kaplan had composed an impassioned dissertation on the sublime force that leads man alone in the animal kingdom to ask any questions at all. True, he had included ten interrogative sentences ending with "he—or she—asked"; but "he" seemed to refer to Jehovah and the "she" to some Biblical ingrate.

"Take your seats, please." Mr. Parkhill glanced at the clock. "Mrs. Tomasic…"

Mrs. Tomasic read her words as if they were caged birds, and her opposites as if releasing them from captivity.

"Any corrections?" asked Mr. Parkhill.

"Not vun!" cried Mr. Kaplan promptly. "Congradulation, Tomasic!"

Mr. Parkhill cleared his throat. "Very good, Mrs. Tomasic." (It sounded woefully anticlimactic after Mr. Kaplan.)

Felicitations rained upon Mrs. Tomasic from one and all.

"Miss Ziev," said Mr. Parkhill.

With zest Miss Ziev read her words, with zeal her opposites; and—happy to relate—not a shadow of error fell upon either.

"Ziev, you soitinly improvink!" exclaimed Mr. Kaplan. "All arond!"

"Yes," said Mr. Parkhill lamely.

Congratulations (for both her antonyms and her nuptials) showered upon proud Miss Ziev.

"Mr. Plonsky…"

Mr. Plonsky read (from his notes, not the Antipodean board). "'Over…under. Save…spend. Strong … wick.'"

Up went the hand of Miss Mitnick. "Mistake!"

"Yes?" (Mr. Parkhill could always rely on Rose Mitnick.)

"The opposite 'strong' is spelled wrong," she said.

"A ragular poet," scoffed Mr. Kaplan, *sotto voce*.

"And how *should* the opposite of 'strong' be spelled?" asked Mr. Parkhill quickly, looking right at Miss Mitnick and ignoring Mr. Kaplan.

" 'W-e-a-k,' " said Miss Mitnick.

"Exactly!" Mr. Parkhill smiled. Mr. Kaplan's face fell. " 'Weak,' Mr. Plonsky, is not 'w*i*ck.' " He wrote "weak" on the board. "You see, class, why we must be so careful in pronunciation? The short 'i' is *not* the long 'e,' and—er—vice-versa. That is what is at the root of Mr. Plonsky's difficulty....Now, who can tell us what 'w*i*ck' means?"

Before anyone could so much as make a stab at what "w-i-c-k" meant, Mr. Kaplan sang out, "Point of order!"

Mr. Parkhill looked up in surprise. He was not accustomed to hearing formality enlisted, nor precedence sought, in the beginners' grade. "Y-yes?"

"Didn't you jost sad 'vick' is wronk?" Mr. Kaplan inquired, puzzled.

"I said that '*wick*' is a perfectly good word—"

"So 'wick' isn't wrong!" Mr. Plonsky cut in righteously. "Just different."

"Well, it is wrong as the opposite of—"

"It's wronk *an*' different!" said Mr. Kaplan sternly. (Put that way, Mr. Plonsky was guilty of two errors instead of one.)

"Teacher said 'wick' is a real woid!" protested Mr. Plonsky.

"So is 'pastrami'!" retorted Mr. Kaplan. "But it's not de opposite 'stronk'!"

Mr. Plonsky clutched his forehead, yammering.

"Gentlemen—!" Mr. Parkhill tapped his chalk on

the board decisively. "We can dispense with—er—sarcasm. Let us return to the question I asked. Who can tell us the meaning of 'wick'?"

Earnest brows furrowed as earnest eyes focused on "wick"; grave lips tightened as grave minds probed for "wick"'s inmost secret. The clock ticked its unalterable toll.

"It's quite a—er—*common* word," said Mr. Parkhill hopefully.

Up went the intrepid hand of Hyman Kaplan.

Mr. Parkhill pretended not to see it. "*Any*one?" he asked anxiously.

No one responded to "Anyone?" except Mr. Kaplan, who began to swing his arm like a pendulum.

Mr. Parkhill adjusted his spectacles. "Mr. Kaplan."

"Saven days make vun—"

"No, no, *no*!" exclaimed Mr. Parkhill severely. "That is '*week*'!" He was quite cross with Mr. Kaplan, and so adamant in applying the chalk that it broke. "Sorry." With a fresh stick he wrote firmly:

> Week
> Weak
> Wick

"My!" Mr. Kaplan murmured admiringly. "I fond a toid void!"

" 'Week,' " said Mr. Parkhill, picking up the pointer and indicating the top word, "means seven days. But 'weak' means—er—not strong. And 'wick'"—he tapped the third word—"is the cord or thread inside a candle, the part that burns!"

A chorus of joy came from his listeners.

"Oooh!"

"So!"

"Vell, haddaya like?!"

It was ever thus: The revelation of a new word was like the establishment of yet another beachhead on the fearsome shores of English. And revelation was always followed by pragmatic test.

"Like in mine cigrat lighter, I have a w*i*ck!" said Miss Gidwitz.

"*Wi*ck, weak, w*ee*k," practiced Mr. Scymzak.

"W*eak*, week, w*i*ck," intoned Miss Tarnova, a jaded whippoorwill.

Mr. Parkhill beamed (how sweet the wine of pedagogy, how heady the draught of success) and called upon Peter Studniczka.

Mr. Studniczka clutched his shirt (he was not wearing a tie this night) and, eyes glassy, read: " 'Black...white. White...black. One...two. Eat...not eat,' " and slumped back into his seat, exhausted.

Before Mr. Parkhill could offer a word of balm or comfort to poor Mr. Studniczka, Mr. Plonsky, smarting under his wounds, lashed out, "What kind opposite is that '*not* eat'?"

"Emoigency kine!" said Mr. Kaplan, rushing to the defense of his ward. "You expact a hongry man should use poifick gremmar?"

"Who said anything about diet?" cried Mr. Plonsky in confusion.

Mr. Kaplan polished his nails piously.

"But 'not eat,' " stammered Miss Mitnick, "isn't an *opposite*!"

"Vy not?" demanded Mr. Kaplan.

"Because—"

"Ha! 'Becawss' isn't a rizzon. It's a conjonction!"

Miss Mitnick flinched.

"*Mr.* Kaplan!" said Mr. Parkhill sternly, and without the slightest effort to conceal his displeasure. "Mr. Plonsky and Miss Mitnick are quite right. 'Not eat' is *not* an opposite. It is, I'm sorry to say, not a good phrase in any sense." He erased "not eat" with one firm swipe of the eraser. "Mr. Plonsky, what *is* the opposite of 'eat'?"

Mr. Plonsky blinked blankly. "Eh…uh…ah…"

"Vell, vell," crooned Mr. Kaplan, "Studniczka at least didn't gargle."

Mr. Plonsky searched for Mr. Kaplan fiercely through his glasses. "Maybe *you* know the opposite 'eat'?"

"*I*," said Mr. Kaplan with dignity, "vasn't called on by Mr. Pockheel!"

"Stop!" gulled Plonsky bleated.

"The opposite of 'eat,'" announced Mr. Parkhill in a loud, if reluctant, tone, "may be one of several words …" He wrote "fast" and "starve" on the board. (It was sometimes hard to know *what* to do about Mr. Kaplan. One could not, after all, tell a full-grown man to stand in the corner.) "And Mr. Studniczka, since 'black' is the opposite of 'white,' 'white' is obviously the—er—opposite of 'black.' You really should have given us one more word and opposite."

He glanced toward the clock unhappily. Mr. Kaplan's opposites were next. *Sauve qui peut.* "Mr. Kaplan," he said deliberately, "before I call upon you, may I remind you that the assignment called only for five words and five opposites? I did *not* want an essay, nor an elaborate—er—introduction."

For once, Mr. Kaplan did not respond to criticism as if it were capital punishment. He did not even act wounded. He was too absorbed in rising, too beguiled by the prospect of reciting, too entranced by the vistas of debate that lay ahead.

"Just read your *words*," warned Mr. Parkhill.

"Only de voids?" asked Mr. Kaplan incredulously. "Not mine *ideas*?" His expression was that of an Alcibiades who could not believe that Socrates would deliberately stab philosophy in the back.

"Only—the—words," repeated Mr. Parkhill, un-moved.

Mr. Kaplan blinked, pondered man's inhumanity to man, bowed to *force majeure*, and, summoning support from the innermost arsenals of his faith, read bravely: "'Fife opposites fromm Hyman Keplen!'" (Exposition, apparently, did not fall into the category of "ideas.") "'Spic...span,'" he recited sadly. "'Tall...shrimp,'" he continued proudly. "'Naut Caroline...Sot Caroline. Op...don. Nightmare...daymare,'" he concluded with the wistfulness of parting.

"*Hanh*?" cried Mr. Blattberg.

"—!" came from Miss Tarnova.

"Psssh!" grinned Mr. Pinsky, slapping his cheek in admiration for his laird.

Miss Mitnick's mouth fell open; her cheeks were bloodless; she was stunned.

Mr. Parkhill was scrutinizing the board in con-sternation. There it was, all right: "Nightmare...day-mare." He ran a finger under his collar. He wished he had opened the window a bit wider. He saw hands, pencils, notebooks, rulers waving wildly in the stratosphere. He heard cries, pleas, petitions ("Mr. Parkhill!" "Titcher!"

149

"Mistake! Mistake!") clamor in the air.

"Class…" he said automatically. "Mr. Kaplan—er—you may sit down."

Mr. Kaplan, who had been rooted to the scene of desire and disappointment, sat down.

"Class, you may lower your hands and—er—objects. Everyone will have a turn….We shall take up Mr. Kaplan's mistakes one at a time."

The last tints of color deserted Mr. Kaplan's cheeks. Not "Mr. Kaplan's mistake" but "Mr. Kaplan's mis*takes*…" And "Everyone will have a turn…" And "one at a time…"! Mr. Kaplan roused himself from depression to face the charge of the Philistines.

The charge wasted no time in charging.

Mr. Plonsky declared vengefully that since "spic" was not the opposite of "span," "span" could not be dragooned into masquerading as the opposite of "spic". "'Spic *and* span,'" said Mr. Plonsky acidly, "can't be broken op. They are like tvins from Siam!"

So felicitous was the phrasing, so vivid the imagery, that the entire Plonsky-Mitnick axis burst into applause.

The exultation had scarcely died down before Stanislaus Wilkomirski was declaiming that "shrimp" could not, by even the most generous canons of usage, be accepted as the opposite of "tall." A shrimp, Mr. Wilkomirski concluded, was a fish, and no fish could be an opposite—"even from Mr. Kaplan!"

A round of guffaws attested to the sweetness of revenge by those who had long suffered at Mr. Kaplan's hands.

Now Olga Tarnova—feline and mysterious—undulated into action: "Is not true thot most aducated people consider North Cahrolina, also South Cahrolina, are *names*? So how can be one opposite other? Could Pinsk be opposite Minsk?" she murmured with wicked irony. Could Christmas be the opposite of New Year's? "Fooey!" (That was the way Miss Tarnova, in a burst of emotion, put it.)

Now the ranks were beside themselves with jubilation.

Even shy Miss Mitnick lost her penguin air of apology, as she took her turn in the lists. "Nightmare—*day*mare?" Her cheeks were flushed. "I can't believe! Who ever heard from a 'daymare'?" She could not finish, so loud was the hilarity of her legions. Mr. Blattberg was holding his sides. Mr. Plonsky was wiping his eyes. Miss Goldberg celebrated with a marzipan raspberry.

Mr. Parkhill had been so busy crossing out Mr. Kaplan's mistakes and substituting antonyms fit for their duties that he had not noticed what effect the relentless cannonade was having on that proud and insular spirit. "Quite right, Miss Mitnick," he said. "There is, strictly speaking, *no* opposite for 'nightmare.' When one does not have a nightmare, one simply has—er—untroubled sleep." He drew three implacable lines through "daymare" and turned. "Are you quite clear about all these corrections, Mr. Kaplan?"

Mr. Kaplan did not respond. He did not, in fact, even seem to *hear*. He was gaping at the board with the haunted and inaccessible expression of one shell shocked. So many corrections—on what had seemed so spic-and-span a text...So much ridicule from such plebeian souls. Mr. Kaplan was mortified. Mr. Kaplan was crushed. There could be no doubt about it: Defeat —massive and incontestable—had come to Hyman Kaplan at last.

"Mr. Kaplan…" Mr. Parkhill repeated.

Mr. Kaplan seemed as bereft of speech as of hearing.

Mr. Parkhill felt a twinge of remorse. Perhaps he should have intervened. Perhaps he should have diluted the ferocity with which the Javerts had pounced upon their Valjean. He felt a pang of guilt. He could have found *some* way of saving Mr. Kaplan's face. At the moment, that face seemed in the throes of death.

The big bell boomed in the corridors. "That will be all for tonight," sighed Mr. Parkhill. He had never seen the class so happy. They were smiling, grinning, chuckling, chortling—riding the sweet, rare rollers of revenge. Some of them repeated choice morsels from Mr. Kaplan's Waterloo; others bade him farewell in syllables either condescending or amused. Only Miss Gidwitz offered a crumb of consolation to her Richard; only Mr. Pinsky, fealty undimmed, glared defiance at the infidels.

"Mr. Koplan," purred Miss Tarnova, leaning over the vanquished warrior like a presence out of Gogol, "you made enough mistakes tonight for whole year!"

"You loined a lesson?" mocked Mr. Blattberg.

"Next time don't confuse opposites and shmopposites!" leered Mr. Plonsky, a malicious owl. "Agreed?"

Only then did some forgotten ember flicker in Hyman Kaplan's eye. He rose. *Avito viret honore*. He drew himself erect. He faced the evil Eumenides.

"Agreet?" he echoed disdainfully, a man who might lose a battle but never a war. "No, mine dear Plonsky. Naver. I give you de *opposite* 'agreet.' Nots!"

Mr. Parkhill wondered if he was having a daymare.

H∗Y∗M∗A∗N K∗A∗P∗L∗A∗N,
Ever Eumoirous

It had all begun so innocently. Only when the fume and foam of conflict had settled, many hours later, far, far from the fierce battlefield, was Mr. Parkhill able to retrace the steps through which he had unwittingly opened that strange Pandora's Box.

Yet how could he have known? Perhaps the season had something to do with it. It was nearing the end of the school year, when tempers usually grew shorter and patience sometimes ran out. How had it begun?

Stanislaus Wilkomirski, a steadfast sexton but unpredictable student, had delivered himself of a composition entitled "Why Horses Die All Over," of which the first sentence read:

> Horses are slower as autmobiles, and
> whose use makes horses die.

The "and," of course, was a perfect example of the superfluous conjunction, that grammatical misdemeanor which Professor Otto J. Horkheimer, in his classic on adult education, so aptly called "thwarted subordination."

Mr. Parkhill tapped the errant "and" with his

pointer and explained how, in implying equality between the two clauses, "and" actually vitiated the *sub*ordination Mr. Wilkomirski had obviously intended. "If we simply remove the 'and,'" said Mr. Parkhill, suiting action to thought with a deft swipe of the eraser, "the relationship between the two ideas is corrected." He paused. "Automobiles do not cause horses to—er—die, Mr. Wilkomirski. Did you not mean to say that the automobile *replaces* the horse?"

Mr. Wilkomirski had no qualms about concurring that the automobile replaces, rather than murders, the horse.

"Does anyone see a misspelled word in that sentence?" Mr. Parkhill asked, rather more pointedly than was his wont.

Miss Mitnick raised her hand. "'Automobile.' Should be an 'o' between 't' and 'm'."

"Good." Mr. Parkhill inserted an "o" between the "t" and the "m".

And that, it turned out, was the fatal moment. Yes that innocuous "o" was the spark that triggered a chain reaction such as even the beginners' grade in its stormiest hour had never known. For "automobile," with its Greek and Latin origins, offered Mr. Parkhill a perfect opportunity to give his students a glimpse of etymology, to show them, as Professor Horkheimer had so often stressed, how to make use of languages other than English, languages which, as adults, they already knew and from which they could draw priceless parallels.

"Can anyone tell me *why* there should be an 'o' after the 't'?" asked Mr. Parkhill.

Up went the hand of Hyman Kaplan.

"Yes?"

"Becawss dat's de vay it's spalled!"

Mr. Parkhill did not try to disguise his disappointment. "That, Mr. Kaplan," he said crossly, "does not help a bit."

"Becawss ve nidd a vowel to squeeze in de sond 'o'?" Mr. Kaplan tried again.

Mr. Parkhill gripped the chalk firmly. "N-no." He made a stroke to separate "auto" from "mobile." "Notice, class: 'Automobile' consists of two parts, 'auto' and 'mobile.' The first happens to come from Greek, the second from Latin. Now each of these has a specific meaning. 'Mobile' means moving. 'Auto' is Greek for—"

"Yos! Yos!" Recognition leaped from the throat of Gus Matsoukas, overjoyed by the appearance, so far from Ithaca, of a childhood friend. " 'Auto'—dot means myself."

"Exactly," said Mr. Parkhill, quite pleased. " 'Automobile' means 'self-moving,' moving under its own power, from the Greek—"

"Now we stodying *Grik*?" cried Mrs. Moskowitz in horror. To Mrs. Moskowitz, English was mystery and torment enough; the one thing it did not need was foreign aid-in-confusion from yet another tongue.

"Did the *Griks* invant automobills?" asked Oscar Trabish incredulously "I thought Hanry Fort—"

"Not!" Mr. Matsoukas thundered. " 'Automobile' is Grik! 'Airplane' is Grik! 'Telephone' is Grik! All, all, all Grik!!"

Nationalism, which never lay more than a few inches beneath the explosive surface of the beginners' grade, now raced through the room like a brush fire.

"Matsoukas, leave a few screps for other nations!" shouted Mr. Pinsky.

"Telephones came from Alexander Grayhond Bell!" averred Cookie Kipnis.

"Airplanes are from U.S.," chirped tiny Mrs. Tomasic, touching her crucifix.

"Class, class...Mr. Matsoukas did not mean that the Greeks actually *invented* all these wonderful devices. He meant that the words used to name them are Greek in origin."

"Aahh..." drifted through the room like an elegy.

"Ohh," murmured many in the flush of comprehension.

"A*ha!*" cried Hyman Kaplan, who scorned half-measures.

Respectful faces turned to Mr. Matsoukas, tendering him, as plenipotentiary, the admiration his forebears so richly deserved.

As for the man from Greece, transformed from scapegoat to savant in the twinkling of an eye, he relapsed into his habitual mutterings and assumed an expression that left no doubt in anyone's mind that the proud people who had given mankind Aristotle and Plato, physics and philosophy, could just as easily have invented the telephone, the airplane and heaven knows what else had they but thought it worth applying their minds to such childish ends.

This was too much for Miss Caravello, whose tribal *amour propre* was easily offended. "Anda who giva da world da Art?" she demanded with passion. "Da Music? Da Church? Leonardo?"

Miss Caravello might have gone on for quite a while cataloguing the grandeurs of Rome had not even this brief sampling stung Olga Tarnova's heritage to the quick.

"Rossia, Rossia!" Miss Tarnova moaned in heartfelt

accents. "Tolstoy. Lermontov. Chakhov. Pushk—"

"Michelangelo! Rossini! Dante!"

"Ladies, *ladies*," said Mr. Parkhill, tapping his pointer on the desk, "we can dispense with such heated dialogue...."

"Also Grik!" cried Gus Matsoukas.

"Mr. *Parkhill* is?" Mr. Scymzak, who wanted to be a barber, could not believe his ears.

" 'Dialogue,' not teacher," snorted Mr. Matsoukas.

"Ha come you know so much Grik and so little English?" asked Mr. Pinsky in amazement.

"He is a man of high colture!" snapped Mr. Plonsky, seizing the opportunity to deflate Mr. Kaplan's first grenadier.

"Ha!" That was Mr. Kaplan. "Jost heppens Matsoukas got *born* in Grik—"

" '*Greece*,' Mr. Kaplan, not 'Grik.' "

"—so for dat he desoives spacial cradit? *T'ink*, Plonsky. Use your bren! Averybody got to loin som lengvidge. Grik is Matsoukas' modder's tong. *Dat* kine colture, enyvun got!" He turned to Mr. Pinsky. "Pinsky, show. Spik a few voids Rumanian."

Stout Pinsky uttered a few words in Rumanian.

"Studniczka!" Mr. Kaplan summoned a second underling. "Give a semple."

Peter Studniczka uttered cryptic syllables from some indecipherable, but no doubt ancient, tongue.

"Gidvitz, say a few voids—"

But Mr. Parkhill was drumming his pencil on his desk most resolutely. "That will do, Mr. Kaplan. Quiet....Suppose we return to 'automobile.' I was merely trying to point out that English is a living language. It is not fixed and unchanging. It grows all the time, adding new words, new shadings—"

"Oy," moaned Mrs. Moskowitz. Poor Mrs. Moskowitz. To her, words were like glaciers, or the oceans; they had always been *there*. To suggest that new words were being spawned right and left around her— that, to Mrs. Moskowitz, was opening the gates to bedlam itself.

"Let's take another word," said Mr. Parkhill quickly, turning to the board, where he printed:

AUTOGRAPH

"Now, class, we saw that 'auto' refers to self. Does anyone know what 'graph' means?"

"Matsoukas, tell," Mr. Kaplan sighed. "You de only Grik in de cless."

Mr. Matsoukas knit his brows. "'Graph'…Yos! *'Grapho.'* Write."

"Good!" said Mr. Parkhill. "Therefore, 'autograph' means one's own writing, one's signature. Now do you see, class?"

They not only saw; they were staggered.

"Ooo…" crooned Miss Tarnova.

"Hadaya like that?"

"Claver!"

"Please, give more examples!"

"There are many, many more examples," said Mr. Parkhill cheerfully. He thought for a moment. "Here is a word which may strike you as—er—hard; yet I'm sure all of you have seen it, dozens of times." On the board, he printed:

HOMOGENIZED

Uncertain murmurs, accompanied by baffled expressions, ascended from the synod of the seated.

"Here is a hint—to the ladies," said Mr. Parkhill. "Whenever you go into a market, I am sure you see—" He touched "homogenized."

"*That?*" cried Mrs. Yanoff. "Naver."

"Who shops in a *zoo?*" asked Cookie Kipnis.

"How we can buy something we can't prononce?" Miss Goldberg reached for the security of a caramel.

Mr. Parkhill was not dismayed. "Think hard, class. I assure you that you have all seen this very word. Many times. Does anyone have a clue?"

The lone hand of Rose Mitnick rose once more. "Doesn't this mean," she blushed, "a certain kind milk?"

"It certainly does!" said Mr. Parkhill heartily. "Homogen—"

"Milk!" cried Mrs. Tomasic.

"Ufcawss!"

"Soitinly!"

"Goodness sek!" mused Miss Ziev, making a note that would enliven many a dinner after she was Mrs. Andrassy.

"I knew you would recognize it," beamed Mr. Parkhill. "Now, 'homogenized' will take on a much richer meaning once we understand what its separate parts *mean*." He raised his chalk and bisected "homogenized." " 'Homo' means 'like,' 'the same.' 'Genos' refers to 'type' or 'kind.' Homogenized milk, therefore, is milk which is the same throughout, in which the cream has been distributed—"

"You mean *I am drinking Grik milk?*" exclaimed Mrs. Moskowitz, scandalized.

"Grik milk is from goats!" growled Mr. Matsoukas.

"*I* am not a goat!"

"You not a cow eider," said Mr. Kaplan sternly, "still you drink American milk!"

At this point, Carmen Caravello, who was becoming increasingly antipathetic to the Hellene, broke in to ask Mr. Parkhill whether Greek was the *only* language which had enriched the Anglo-Saxon; had not a certain other noble tongue endowed its linguistic treasures to English? Through both her question and her intonation, which suggested an overheated diplomat delivering an icy *démarche*, Miss Caravello practically accused Mr. Parkhill of playing favorites among the nations.

"Latin," Mr. Parkhill agreed at once, "has probably contributed even more words to English than Greek has."

"*Bravo*," said Miss Caravello simply.

"Still *anodder* lengvidge?" moaned Mrs. Moskowitz.

"My nephew write Latin for medicine," Mr. Scymzak confided. "He is doctor."

"Suppose we try a few words with Latin roots...." On the board, Mr. Parkhill printed:

POSTPONE

"Now, 'post' means 'after,' and 'pone' comes from 'pono'—'place.' So 'post-pone' means—"

"Tea!" came an eager voice.

Mr. Parkhill stopped short. "I beg your pardon?"

"Tea!" It was blinking Plonsky. "A Chinee woid."

"Oh, I see what you mean. Why, yes. 'Tea' is, I believe, from the Chinese—"

"Zwieback!"

Mr. Parkhill coughed. "I beg—"

"Zwieback!" Mr. Guttman insisted. "From Cher-many!"

"Yes—"

"Menalife," mused Mr. Kaplan, posed like Rodin's Thinker. "Aren't eny voids in English fromm *England*?"

"England? Pah!" throbbed Olga Tarnova, all scorn. "England is not romahnteek. Sail-boys and bonkers. Rossia! Rossia gives beautifulest words!"

That was all that was needed to rouse those who carried the Mediterranean in their blood.

"*Per carita!*"

"Rossian..." sneered Mrs. Rodriguez.

"Give example!" challenged Mr. Matsoukas.

"Blintzes!" retorted Olga Tarnova. "Cahviar. Vodka."

"Dose are *names*, not voids!" protested Mr. Kaplan.

"Tschaikowsky! Blini! Borsht!"

"Miss Tarnova—"

"All, all Rossian!"

"But dey *stay* Rossian!" stormed Mr. Kaplan. "Ve vant voids vhich *pess* from vun lengvidge into anodder. Kipp your borsht an' blintzes! Can you *homogenize* somting in Rossian?" (Mr. Matsoukas, finding an unexpected champion among those he had always considered Trojan at heart, gave the Athenian equivalent of "Hear, hear.") "Did dey name a talephone, a hot drink, iven a cold sneck—"

"Class—"

"You are prajudiced against Rossia!" railed Miss Tarnova, dabbing at her eyes.

"He'sa jalous Latin, too!" chimed in Miss Caravello.

"We must be *broad*-mind," Miss Mitnick put in plaintively. "Mr. Kaplan, you are not international—"

"Ha! I'm not a Chinaman eider, but I didn't object to

161

Plonsky's 'tea'!"

Mr. Parkhill was frowning so severely, and rapping his pointer so sternly, that he stilled the inflamed factions by sheer will. "We really *must* not let ourselves be carried away by our emotions, class. Nothing is to be gained by these—er—exchanges. We are here to study, not argue." Stigmata of shame appeared on the features of his followers. "Since some of us seem to feel so intensely about this," he remarked dryly, "I suggest that those of you who wish to may bring to our next session a brief list of words you recognize as being of—er—foreign derivation."

And that was how it had begun. Just that simply. Who could have foreseen that Mr. Parkhill's parting words would open the dikes to a flood?

For that was precisely the way Mr. Parkhill felt now—flooded, inundated by wave upon wave of words, names, roots, prefixes, suffixes, rolling across the classroom from distant and exotic shores. No sooner had he finished calling the roll than Mrs. Rodriguez, who must have consulted half the Spanish-speaking population of New York, started rattling off words of Hispanic vintage like a machine gun, beginning with "arena," ending with "tobacco," and including at least five extrapolations of "cigar."

Mrs. Rodriguez had scarcely run out of breath before Mr. Matsoukas, who seemed to have plundered Homer and Euripides, began flinging gems from the Aegean before the barbarians. No sooner had the dust settled in Mr. Matsoukas' path than Carmen Caravello was pouring out melodious syllables culled from the Tyrol to Calabria.

And before *her* last, ringing echoes had died in the fervent air, Olga Tarnova, bosom heaving, bracelets jangling, eyes smoldering with strictly retroactive love of Holy Russia (civilization had been murdered in 1917, as far as Miss Tarnova was concerned), began to intone her Slavic litany.

Mr. Parkhill had seen nothing like it, even in the American Night Preparatory School for Adults.

Mr. Guttman followed Miss Tarnova with proud extracts from the tongue of Goethe, ranging from "edelweiss" to "pumpernickel." Mrs. Tomasic donated several reverent vocables from some Balkan clime, which, since no one could understand them, joined the ranks of English without challenge. Mr. Trabish offered two words which bore Israel's proud *imprimatur*, "kibitzer" and "mish-mash," to which Cookie Kipnis, a more fastidious spirit, added "babel," "bagel" and "lox." Mr. Wilkomirski nobly rose above the call of Poland to present words from three languages in which he had not the slightest vested interest: "carnival," "whiskey," "omelet."

The room was beginning to resemble the Olympic Games.

Now Mr. Kaplan, who had remained suprisingly mute throughout the etymological parade, finally managed to catch Mr. Parkhill's eye. He did this with an obbligato of humming and a beseeching mooniness of visage which implied that he might die on the spot unless recognized.

It proved unnecessary for Mr. Parkhill to do so, because Mr. Kaplan, divining the intent, anticipated the act: He leaped to his feet, announced "Have I got beauriful voids!," bestowed a pitying glance upon those whom, through silence, he had seduced into preceding him (Mr. Kaplan had the instincts of a Belasco where timing was concerned), and strode front and center.

All the other students had recited from their seats, Mr Parkhill observed; but to ask Mr. Kaplan to renounce the spotlight, or forfeit the advantages which accrue to an erect speaker addressing a semi-recumbent audience, was like asking Jupiter to abandon Olympus.

"Frands, fallow-students, all-Amaricans!" Mr. Kaplan beamed. (Mr. Pinsky promptly returned it with compound interest.) "I say 'all-Amaricans' becawss only in a school in vunderful Amarica could ve see such pridte in accomplishmants fromm *odder* nations! In dis megnificent etmosphere—"

"*Mr.* Kaplan," Mr. Parkhill broke in, "this is not an exercise in Recitation and Speech."

"Who denies?"

"Then may I suggest you simply present your foreign words?"

"I shouldn't give *beckgrond remocks*?" Mr. Kaplan looked like Apollo being asked to discard his lyre.

"No," said Mr. Parkhill, quite frostily. "There is no need whatever for back*ground*, not 'grond,' rem*a*rks, not 'remocks.'"

Mr. Kaplan might just as well have been cashiered out of the regiment. He glanced upward, appealing to the goddess with the blindfold, picked up a piece of chalk, released a sigh which wedded injury to innocence, capped it with a shrug which soothed pain with forbearance, and, with a brave lift of the eyebrows, printed nine letters on the board:

EUMOIROUS

Mr. Parkhill felt as if he were in an elevator whose cable has snapped.

"*Vat?*" That was outraged Blattberg.

"Is that a woid or a disease?" That was angry Scymzak.

"Some people got a noive like gall stones!" That was seething Yanoff, ominous in black.

"Mr. Kaplan, I—er—"

Mr. Kaplan did not shift his feet or his gaze by so much as a centimeter.

"Fake! A fake woid!" That was righteous Plonsky.

"Watch out for his treecks!" That was callous Tarnova.

" 'Eumoi—' oy!" That was Mrs. Moskowitz.

"Class…" Mr. Parkhill felt miserable. In all his years in the American Night Preparatory School for Adults, no student had ever brought into the classroom, from the world beyond, a word he could not explain: Mr. Kaplan had bagged a specimen Mr. Parkhill could not even *recognize*. His eyes bored into the nine letters before him. What an ungainly word, an outlandish word, a Grecian freak. Mr. Parkhill doubted that the Greeks themselves had ever used it.

"Eumoirous…eumoirous…" It raced through Mr. Parkhill's head, faster and faster, like a player in musical chairs frantically hunting for a seat. The prefix, of course, meant "good"; and "moir"—perhaps from "moira"—something to do with destiny. "Euphorious" popped into his mind. Could Mr. Kaplan possibly have meant "eu*phor*ious" instead of "eu*moir*ous"? There was, after all, a good deal about Mr. Kaplan that was emphatically euphorious.

"*Where you got such crazy woid?*" he heard Mr. Plonsky roar.

"Vhere?" Mr. Kaplan raised a regal arm and pointed to the stand on which Webster's Unabridged Dictionary reposed. "Dere."

"Som Keplen, ha?" Mr. Pinsky chortled to one and all.

Mr. Plonsky put his head between his hands and moaned.

"Mr. Kaplan," said Mr. Parkhill carefully, "suppose you tell us what that word—er—means."

"It's Grik," said Mr. Kaplan.

This laconicism only fanned the wrath of his opponents, who were not to be hamstrung tonight.

"*Noo?*"

"Answer!"

"Don't dock the quastion!"

"Mr. Kaplan," said Mr. Parkhill, "we do not doubt that your word is Greek. But that is *not* what I asked you. I want to know what the word *means*."

"Don't *you* know?" asked Mr. Kaplan in astonishment.

"No," said Mr. Parkhill firmly. He would not dissemble; he would not evade; these, in a teacher, were heinous sins. And yet, the moment he uttered the fatal negative, Mr. Parkhill regretted it. He regretted it for two reasons: (1) he had walked right into an ambush, in which Mr. Kaplan had cunningly transferred the burden of elucidation from his own shoulders to Mr. Parkhill's, and (2) the whole class was staring at him—their Solomon, their Solon—as if the very foundations upon which education rested were crumbling before their eyes.

"*Teacher* don't know a word?" asked Stanislaus Wilkomirski, dazed.

166

"A foreigner can stomp an American-born?" asked Miss Ziev, aghast. (She kept fingering her engagement ring, as if to remind herself that not all was lost.)

"Mr. Parkhill..." wan Mitnick, bewildered, could say no more.

They were like believers whose shaman has lost his powers of divination; passengers on a storm-tossed ship whose captain has just confessed a total ignorance of navigation.

"Class..." Mr. Parkhill adjusted his spectacles, teetered back and forth on his heels, fighting for time. "Let us not make mountains out of molehills. No one knows or uses all the words in English. There are, after all, half a million words in the language—" A "*Gewalt!*" came from Mrs. Moskowitz, whose nerves collapsed at half a hundred. "—and no one can possibly keep all of them in his head. That, in fact, is one of the reasons we *have* dictionaries!"

He saw relief creep into Mr. Pinsky's features, life return to Miss Mitnick's cheeks. The tide was turning in his favor. His sheep were regaining their shepherd. "Now, Mr. Kaplan," he said sternly, "will you please proceed? Define 'eumoirous.' "

Strangely enough, Mr. Kaplan did not look ecstatic, as might be expected in one who had achieved the unprecedented feat of stumping Mr. Parkhill. Mr. Kaplan did not even look content. He looked like Boswell, had he inadvertently sent Dr. Johnson sprawling in the dust. Mr. Kaplan lifted a slip of paper, from which he dolorously read: " 'Eumoirous. Adjective.' It minns: 'Heppy or fortunate from de goodness of vun's inclinations an' ections. " He lowered the paper.

A censorious hiss slithered forth from Olga Tarnova.

"Shame, shame on such a word!"

"*I* wouldn't make Mr. Parkhill troubles!" averred Miss Pomeranz.

"Give yourself already a diploma and greduate from the school!" called Mr. Plonsky caustically, from between tragic hands.

Not a retort or demurrer or *riposte* came from Hyman Kaplan's lips. He stood in stoic silence.

"Well, class," Mr. Parkhill began, "Mr. Kaplan has brought us a—er—most rare word."

Mr. Plonsky turned to Mr. Pinsky tauntingly. "What's a matter, corporal, why you look pale? You are maybe ashamed of General Keplan?"

"Criticize Keplen, not Pinsky!" flared Mr. Kaplan.

"So *you* be ashamed! Bringing in a crazy fency word—"

"Keplen is *prod*, not ashamed! How ve vill loin if ve don't try de onusual?!"

"Your woid is not unusual; it is onbelievable!" bellowed Mr. Plonsky.

"So blame Grik, not Keplen!" shrugged his scourge.

"Kaplan, give already one *inch*," Bessie Shimmelfarb pleaded as of yore.

"Gentlemen—"

"You not fair, Mr. Kaplan," wailed Miss Mitnick. "Mr. Parkhill wanted words would *help*, not confuse—"

"Som pipple," said Mr. Kaplan, narrowing his orbs, "can drown in a gless of vater."

"But all others in class gave *useful* words—"

"Aducation doesn't have to be useful!"

"But in a hundred *years* we wouldn't use a word like 'eumoirous'!" complained Miss Mitnick tearfully.

"Could heppen an occasion vill arise to *som* student who might use 'eumoirous' any minute!"

"The day you use this cuckoo woid," stormed Mr. Plonsky, "snakes will fly and alephants sing!"

"Keplen," said Mr. Kaplan loftily, "is not responsible for de enimal kingkom."

Mr. Plonsky began talking to himself.

"Mr. Kaplan!" Mr. Parkhill did not even try to soften his tone. "I must say I entirely agree with Miss Mitnick and Mr. Plonsky. Your word is *most* obscure. Good English is simple English. The purpose of words is to communicate, not to impress."

As Mr. Parkhill went on, Mr. Kaplan's features began to sag, like wax under heat. He had expected Mr. Parkhill to praise him for discovering so rare a creature as "eumoirous," perhaps even cite him for audacity in bringing it to bay. Instead, Launcelot, sorely besieged, discovered King Arthur leading the Saracens.

"Now let us turn to an exercise on dangling participles." Mr. Parkhill picked up the textbook thoughtfully. "Page sixty-five. Mr. Kaplan..." That crushed poet had remained rooted to the scene of his disaster. "You—er—you may resume your seat."

For the rest of the evening, Mr. Kaplan sat silent, stunned, wrapped in desolation. Great Achilles had retired to the tent of pride, and within it—who knew his thoughts? Only as the hour of departure drew nigh did Mr. Kaplan bestir himself—and then it was only to bend head over notebook and, without sound or sign, write steadily.

The terminal bell tolled. The warriors filed out of the room, weary but enlightened, trailing the familiar pleasantries of farewell.

"Good night, Mr. Parkhill."

"Goot ivning."

"So lonk!" Mr. Blattberg almost struck Miss Gursky with the baby teeth on the end of the gold chain he was twirling.

Mr. Parkhill collected his books and papers. He noticed that Mr. Kaplan was still seated, writing. Mr. Parkhill made a little more noise than necessary in closing his desk drawer.

Mr. Kaplan rose. "Goot night." He said it with great dignity.

"Good night," said Mr. Parkhill.

The portal closed.

Mr. Parkhill leaned back in his chair and massaged his temples. It had been a most trying night. He felt vexed. Greek and Roman roots had promised so much....He remembered that Professor Horkheimer had written an entire and excellent chapter on "Words to Aid Us from Foreign Lands"—but Professor Horkheimer had obviously never been obliged to confront a certain kind of problem, or contend with a certain kind of student.

Mr. Parkhill noticed a paper on his desk. It was an ordinary sheet of foolscap, folded once. He unfolded it. Something was written on it, upside down. He turned it right side up, and read:

> Dear Mr. Parkhill
>   Tonight I disagreet with you.
>   Still, you are the best teacher.
>   If I don't learn from you, I won't learn from anyone.
>   (singed)
>   Hyman Kaplan
> p.s. Tonight you should feel eumoirous.

170

That was just like Mr. Kaplan! To find a way, however strained, however involved, to prove his point, to win the last and incontestable word. "Eumoirous...Happy from the goodness of one's inclinations and actions." Well, Mr. Parkhill did not feel at all eumoirous.

He put on his coat and hat before some echo of meaning, some delayed awareness of incongruity, made him pause. "Singed, Hyman Kaplan." Why, Mr. Kaplan had spelled his name without stars! Without colors! Without red letters outlined in blue and garnished with stars of green!

Mr. Parkhill picked up the foolscap page again. On the underside of the fold, which he had not seen before, was printed:

TO MR. P*A*R*K*H*I*L*L

As he snapped the lights out, Mr. Parkhill wondered whether, in all the years he hoped lay before him, he would ever again be so honored.

He felt eumoirous.